THE UTOPIA OF US

An anthology inspired by
Yevgeny Zamyatin's *We*

Edited by Teika Marija Smits

Introduction © Teika Marija Smits 2024
Stories © is with each individual author 2024
Cover Design © Francesca T Barbini 2024
Cover Image © Teika Marija Smits 2023

Editorial Team Francesca T Barbini and Teika Marija Smits

First published by Luna Press Publishing, Edinburgh, 2024

www.lunapresspublishing.com

ISBN-13: 978-1-915556-45-5

For Andre, who set me on the path of editing this anthology,
and for Francesca, who made the journey so smooth
and enjoyable.

And in memory of my wonderful friend Christopher Priest
who offered to write a story for this anthology.

Sadly, time ran out.

Contents

Introduction

An Old Friend's Recommendation – Umbrella – The Stillness of Falling Snow

A few years ago, on Facebook, I wrote about some of my favourite books, citing *1984* as a novel that had long fascinated me. An old friend from university commented on my post, wondering if I'd read Yevgeny Zamyatin's *We* – the inspiration for Orwell's *1984*. Although I was distantly aware of *We*, my friend's recommendation gave me the nudge I needed to finally buy myself a copy.

I have a very distinct memory of where I was when I first started reading the novel. It was a cold winter's day, and I was standing outside my son's primary school, waiting to pick him up for lunch, the newly bought book in my coat pocket. It had just begun to snow, so I opened the brightly coloured golf umbrella I'd taken with me. As I read the opening of the novel, I was transported to another world. A world I vaguely knew from my Russian mother's life experiences; the anecdotes of my Latvian father who had also spent time in the Soviet Union. It was both *1984* and not *1984*. It was every dystopian film I'd watched, and yet so much deeper, richer. It was also poetic, passionate and absurd. In other words, very Russian. As the snow fell around me, I was conscious of the quiet; the stillness of this beautiful moment.

Of course, the practicalities of life intruded and broke the magic, yet *We* had cast its spell on me and so in every free moment I returned to Zamyatin's world. When I came to the end of the book, I was aware that I wasn't really finished with it. Or rather, it had not finished with me. Later, when I realised that 2024 would be the centenary of its first publication, I knew I had to somehow mark this important anniversary. Having previously edited a number of speculative fiction anthologies, the way forward was obvious. Thus the idea of *The Utopia of Us* was conceived, and I was delighted when Francesca Barbini of Luna Press Publishing agreed to take on the project.

The response to the call for submissions was incredible – there was so much enthusiasm for the concept of the collection. Reading the submissions was a real pleasure, and bringing together both the chosen stories from the open call and the stories from commissioned authors a creatively enriching process. As always when collating an anthology, I was intrigued to see the connections between the stories: the overlap in themes, tone and voice. Yet each author's story is unique and compelling in its own way. I'd like to think that I've helped to recreate – at least, in part – a little something of my experience of first reading *We*. I hope these stories transport you; bring a stillness, a hushed beauty, to your day. Most of all, I hope that this anthology inspires more people to discover Zamyatin's ground-breaking novel.

Teika Marija Smits, March 2024

Intrinsic – Extrinsic – Terrific

Aliya Whiteley

I am U914, and I write to those above.

The underground system is a marvel of the United State. It takes the numbers wherever they need to go: to work, to live, as tools within our magnificent society. But I wonder how many, riding the transit, sitting in their own thoughts of the day ahead or just passed, have spared time to consider the role of the underground worker? Perhaps they have glanced at a driver. Those who lead the way, steer our paths, are often lauded, and rightly so. I only humbly ask that we think of those who maintain those paths. The diggers, the layers of track. And so many jobs beyond that. Or rather, below that.

My job was explained to me as thus:

The act of travel has long been observed to encourage a loquacious quality, a dissolution of social barriers in those who undertake even short trips, and this can lead to inappropriate interactions. Those surface numbers who use the underground system can be encouraged to keep their barriers intact. Every transit contains monitoring devices. Conversations that are deemed personal in nature are discouraged. Small discrepancies lead to tiny reprimands; every seat is fitted with a prickler. Pricklers deliver the lightest of shocks to the back and thighs, but it is usually enough to change the course of a discussion. *What was that?* some say. *Did you feel that?* Or they fall silent, dissecting what they experienced: a tingling through the seat, or coming from their organs, maybe? A medical issue? They think of doctors, and inner workings. I watch them try to make sense of it, and by the time they've recovered the journey is nearing its end. They disembark and return to the surface and think no more of it until next time. Those who are having mutually excitable conversations might require another level of intervention. Their names are passed to the Bureau of Guardians.

We – underground team UT32 – activate pricklers thousands of times in a single shift. When a shift is done we do not return to the surface. No stepping out into the sunlight, or into the cool breeze of the night. No visiting the places to which the stations lead: the Plaza of the Cube, or the Botanic Gardens. No, we take the elevators down to our living quarters, divided into dormitories, and we sleep until the next shift begins. We are separate from those who live above in every way. Nothing is contaminated with their habits, their feelings. Sometimes I think (whisper it) that we are a purer form of communal existence that they are not yet ready to embrace.

Having said that, it can get cramped down here.

Space is a luxury in the underground life. I have a bed in dormitory U900-988, and some of us do snore, which is a bodily affectation one must bear, but it doesn't always lead to a sunny disposition on shift. I have a regular timeslot, once every twenty shifts, in a private cubicle. I have pink tickets, of course, but I find the work tiring and am rarely in the mood for such interactions. I must admit I try to discourage colleagues from asking for that kind of emotional output from me, mainly by making disparaging comments such as "What a funny old business!" and "Honestly, I don't think that's one of my skill sets." It seems to work. That leaves me free to use my cubicle time to sit alone, and simply enjoy being singular. Sometimes it feels... illicit. I write this down so that you can appreciate that I am fallible too. I am like you. And you are high above, but you are like me. We are linked. We are one.

Sitting at my desk, monitoring the numbers, gives me purpose. Yes, through the rigorous application of the pricklers, but beyond that I have a goal – to help everyone to accept the connections between us. To realise that conversations in which numbers moan about their singular issues, lifestyles, differences, are unhelpful. Is this pride, to think I might be able to find answers to these problems? I cannot say. All I can tell is that there is a strangeness to our society that excites me, and it lies in the difference between what is inside me, what I feel to be true, and what the world presents to me.

Basically speaking: what's this whole being alive business about?

*

I've monitored so many conversations. The speakers are part of projects, from all parts of our society, that they consider to be profound. More than that: they think their involvements, their goals, to be *more important* than others. If I was up there, I might agree, but from down here, all such endeavours become a mess of selfish intentions. The ones that seem most misguided, I prickle, and then report.

But they are not all vain and/or delusional.

I first came across I632 when she was travelling, deep in conversation. But she was not speaking to another. She spoke only to herself.

She was speaking about her role as a worker on a rocket ship called Integral.

It was an interesting set of mutterings about how Integral would unite us all. It was not an inwards-focussed speech; no, I632 had her gaze firmly fixed outwards, upwards. Higher. For as she spoke it became clear to me that Integral was nothing less than a craft designed to take the best of the United State spacewards, beyond our barriers, to seek out new places, new opportunities. Finally: a mission that could truly call itself meaningful! I listened to her explain Integral, defend it, laud it. She was passionate, rousing, and yet she spoke to nobody but herself. She barely moved her lips, and kept her eyes cast downwards, never looking into the face of another number. I could make no sense of it. I could not forget it. Well, perhaps I would have forgotten it, if it was not for the fact that my next shift found her on my transit, under my monitor, once more – and she gave the same speech again. Body demure, eyes lowered, mouth barely moving, she spoke, and the devices picked up those words of hope, of belief, of possibility. Integral would be the pinnacle of the United State's achievement. She said it again, and again. Every shift, I found her in the act of repetition. She believed utterly.

Perhaps I should have prickled her, or even reported her to the Bureau of Guardians. Instead, in my next allotted cubicle session, I took out one of my pink tickets (not to request her sexually – no above/below fraternisation is allowed) and wrote on the back of it. I jotted down everything she had said. I repeated it, over and over, in my mind. I memorised it. Then I ate the ticket, and it was as if Integral had entered me, penetrated me, claimed me. It was all I could think about. And still I632 got into the transit, travelled to and from her work, and repeated the words. We were linked in a way that made no sense, could not be explained. I wanted her to know it.

*

I maintain that I have never been bothered by the underground existence. Let me repeat that: it was not the quality of being below others, locked inside the earth, that began to prey on my mind at that point. It was only that, for the first time, living in the above seemed to be a desirable situation. It was Integral that called to me. I felt I understood it. Here is why: it was the bedrock of our society sent skywards: the beauty of the United State in motion. How could I not feel a kinship with its creation and an ecstasy with its existence?

But I felt saddened, too. I experienced the highest highs and lowest lows. I could not bear to be excluded from its mission.

I632 said her speech, over and over. It was more than a speech. It was a declaration. I found myself saying it with her.

It wasn't enough.

*

If the underground system is a body then the transit tunnels are the arteries. There are other tunnels. All dormitories, cubicles and living spaces are linked by smaller networks, veins if you will picture it so, that enable access to maintenance and storage areas, and escape routes too, in the rare event of a collapse. These routes are slim staircases that stretch for miles, and the one at the back of the monitoring office for UT32 – behind a door right next to the comfort facilities – happens to link to a number of station platforms, including the one where 1632 began her journey every day.

It would be easy to take that particular fact as a sign, if one believed in things – an individual peccadillo that deserves more than a few prickles. Beyond the ridiculous business of believing, I do think there's merit in taking advantage of situations that present themselves fortuitously. The idea would never have occurred to me if the escape route hadn't been an alive, organic link between our geographical locations.

I took my usual bathroom break. It was easy to slip away, take the door to the left rather than the right, and start climbing. The worst part was the pounding of my heart. I had never even considered such an action before; I was the watcher, not one who needed watching! Every time another number passed me by I felt certain they would see my sweating brow, and hear my heart at work, louder than the transits roaring overhead.

It took an age, but I reached the door to the platform, and slipped through.

The platform was long, and brightly lit, and filled with surface numbers whose faces were blank, focussed on the shifts ahead of them. On the monitoring device they had looked… different, somehow. Flatter. Now I could see that they were like me, and I wondered what had singled me out as suitable for UT work. I had been a child when the routine procedural tests had indicated a certain flexibility in my persona to things others consider a necessity: daylight, and space. I had willingly left the child-rearing factory and gone down into the underground life, and prided myself upon it. Why? There was no answer to that internal question. I walked along the platform, searching for 1632, unsure if I would even recognise her in this new, strange, 3D world.

There she was: one of a crowd, but somehow separate. She was superior to them all, in mission and bearing. She was perfectly alive. I stood behind her, slightly to the side. Her lips were moving. She was already in the act of recitation. Her physical form surprised me; she was really quite short, and rounded. Her shoulders were broad and her cheeks fuller. Everything about her had been shrunken by the monitoring device, but in reality, she was puffed up, like a balloon: filled with air and thought and feeling.

The transit arrived, and everyone surged forward, slipping through the sliding doors, finding a seat. 1632 took the one she preferred, in the corner. Luck was with me. I sat beside her. She glanced in my direction, then away.

The doors slid shut, and the transit began its journey. Three stops until she disembarked. Eight minutes. There was no reason to think my absence had been noticed. Nobody was watching. Nobody had a finger on the prickler.

"I live here," I said. I pitched the volume carefully, and looked at the other numbers, sitting across the aisle. They did not react. Neither did 1632. I tried again, a little louder. There. She heard me. I saw her react, tilt her head. She stopped her recitation.

"I live down here, and I work on systems deep below the earth," I said, "and you work on a system that will go far above."

"How do you know that?" she said.

"You say so. Every time you travel."

"Oh, that. The speech." She laughed a little, breathless. "Yes, I do practise it a lot. You've heard it?"

The only way to make the eight minutes count was total honesty. I braced myself, and said, "It's amazing. Inspiring. The glass rocket. Integral."

She nodded. "It's quite something."

"You're so lucky to work on that project. Space flight. The stars."

Her face fell. A serious expression overcame her features,

deflating them. I wished she would laugh again. "You think so?"

"Trust me. I monitor a lot of conversations. The speech you wrote moved me. Brought out the best in me." Was that true? I had so wanted only to say true things.

"I didn't write it," she said. "I was chosen to deliver it. Today. I'm on my way to do it now, to The Innovative Board. It was thought an engineer should deliver it, and I got picked. I don't know why. I worked on the launch thruster design. That's my job. Design."

It had never occurred to me that these weren't her words, her thoughts. She was not as I had imagined her at all.

"Don't get me wrong," she said, quickly, looking at my expression. "I'm honoured to be part of the magnificent project, and I will do my best to inspire and reassure the board."

I'd never heard of the Innovative Board and I thought I'd heard everything. "Reassure them of what?"

She hesitated, pursed her lips. Why should she say more, to a stranger? I thought she would turn her head away, or move seats. But instead she said, "That Integral is the right course of action."

"There's any doubt?"

She fell silent. Then she whispered, "I suspect I'm the wrong person for this task. I don't understand many things. Societal things. I like to design."

It was at that point I realised she did not repeat the words of the speech over and over because she believed in them. She repeated them because she did not believe in them. She had the freedom to deliver such wonderful words, and she did not want it. It was a revelation to me. The transit slowed, came to a stop. The doors slid open. Some numbers departed, and others entered, all in an orderly fashion. The doors closed, and movement began again.

"It's so strange," I told her. I had to tell her. "You don't want to speak today. Every day I listen to such self-centred conversation." I told her a little about the monitoring role. "Nobody says anything important. You say you don't understand – simply spend a little time listening to them, and you'll understand. They are not frightening, or inexplicable. They are not interested in anything but themselves. They are small," I said. "And Integral is large, larger than them all."

"You really believe that?" she asked me. "You sound so certain."

It was as if I had been hit with a great weight in the chest. Yes, I was certain. I wanted to pass my certainty on to others, I wanted nothing more than to go to that conference of Guardians and make them listen to me. How had 1632 put it? To inspire them. To reassure them. To have all the right words at my disposal. Not to wait for somebody else to speak all the wrong words. No punishment. No blame.

"I want to speak," I said. "And you want to listen."

An idea came to me. It was so sudden, in my head, fully formed, complete. I threw away all caution and I told her my plan. I don't think I will ever get over the fact that she agreed to it.

When the transit arrived at her destination it was not 1632 that disembarked. It was not 1632 that stepped out under the clouded sky, into light rain. It was not 1632 that arrived at the meeting of the Innovative Board, and stepped out on to a great stage, with a hundred numbers before her, eyes assessing, ears attuned.

*

Everyone has a purpose in this glorious United State, and even the smallest role is important to the workings of the whole. No project better illustrates this fundamental truth than the rocket ship Integral. Many thousands of small parts will make up the whole, each one the culmination of tiring labour. Diminish one tiny element, and the whole will fall back down to Earth, but join together in intent and meaning, and it will achieve greatness.

Picture Integral, shooting into space, as the giant, raised index finger of our Benefactor, piercing the sky, taking our vision forth! It will be the pinnacle of our collective achievement.

Some may wonder if one small rocket alone is worth the effort, but is the finger worth the hand? Is the hand worth the arm? Is the arm worth the body, and is the body the home of the number? What we do with our extremities expresses our internal strength. We travel from inwards out, from the Earth to the sky, from our separate bodies to our one true spirit. Integral points the way.

Thank you for listening.

*

I stepped off the stage. I felt free. Free of the world. Of gravity. I floated. I had never felt so alive, so completely myself, and yet part of the whole. A United State of being.

A number with a clipboard approached me, and said, "I thought 1632 was meant to be giving this speech?"

"She's indisposed," I said.

"Never mind, you were adequate. The Board will make final funding decisions in a few days. We'll let your team know whether you can move on from the design stage."

Integral: it didn't even exist yet. It was a thought. A concept. I felt myself come back down to Earth, and land with a gentle bump. "Thank you," I said.

*

I am U914. I write to those above, who make the decisions about what courses of action our society should pursue. I write on the back of the pink tickets I will never use. I write for myself, and for everyone else, and I fear I will never speak these words aloud, and nobody will ever hear them.

It seems so odd, now, to think that my plan ever worked.

After I gave the speech I took the transit, slipped through an escape route, and returned to my desk. 1632 was not there. I have no idea if she sat at my desk for a while and listened to conversations. Sometimes I imagine that she did, and she learned something important that day. Maybe she chose to prickle a few numbers, just to see what that was like.

She still takes the transit to and from her job. She never speaks, now. Even if someone sits beside her and tries to make pleasant conversation for a stop or two. I think she's picturing me, listening.

And so I go on, monitoring conversations. Many numbers think themselves important, and maybe they are. But now I listen less for the revelation of their flaws, and more for the validation of their pride. Above, below, up, down, in, out: we are all part of this terrific endeavour.

Here's my great design: a United State Exchange Program. Surface numbers and underground numbers swapping roles, learning about the other, having new ideas that create new realities. Would that be a crime?

Maybe I will eat these tickets, too. Maybe my words should all be kept inside me, until the time when a rocket ship takes us to the stars. I understand 1632 much better now: it is so hard to tell others about the things that are inside us, and to feel anything but fear at the idea that they might actually listen.

Engine – The Blast – Antiques for Okras

R.T. Ester

K.O. died and left me this shack with the hens in the yard. The hens died as well later on. Last one laid an okra before she passed.

At the time, I'd been your grandmamie for only a year, but I'd lived about sixty since I first saw an okra. I must've been as old as you are now. I cried when Mamie cut it up. K.O. used to say okras don't like being cut up, so when you do, they cry tears that stick to everything. He never tried to cut one in his life.

We met after Mamie died. He saw okras too when he was little. He told me he was at the star festival around the time I first attended with Mamie. The thing is, K.O. liked to tell stories like that. He would always say fate brought us together, but not on its first try. He wanted to see a star before he passed. Those hens just wouldn't lay one okra while he looked after them.

The collector from across the big lake comes to visit every few days, and always, he asks to see it. Your grandmamie may be as old as the parts of town under the lake, but I'm still a good shot with K.O.'s rifle. The collector knows he shouldn't try me, so he tries selling me tips on how to preserve it instead, before he's on to the next house.

If I'd lived before the engine blast, I wouldn't have wanted to hear a word from him. Everyone and their mamie has a story about an okra going bad – someone they knew who travelled and came back to find mucus all over it. Those stories can be hard to ignore, even knowing they aren't true.

Okras don't spoil. They also don't come with seeds, so you can't plant them like you would plant cucumbers or hibiscuses. You can only eat them or trade for something else.

What would you trade my okra for, little Shan?

*

A trading company came around when I lived with Mamie, before the year's festival. It was a caravan with just the driver and a merchant whose name I've been happy to forget. I was ten. Mamie would take me to the old harbour and let me run around while she made her roosters do tricks for visitors to the island.

The sign on the caravan read *Antiques for Okras*. It opened on the other side to onlookers who convened under its awning, pointing at items on the display rack, bragging to each other about hens they knew who would soon lay okras, and how they knew, and what items on display they'd be willing to part with those okras for.

The merchant was a boisterous man who liked to get in fights with people just looking around, and maybe he once killed an islander for stealing one of the artifacts he came to trade with. Never confirmed but the thief was buried behind the old chapel and, a few days later, the VCR was back on the rack.

I only know what to call it because Mamie told me later on. Piece of junk, she said. Even before the engine blast, it had been phased out in favour of newer pieces of junk.

I was in the crowd when the merchant lifted another off the rack – maybe even the same one. He hugged it to his chest and his eyes rounded in shock at the woman insisting it was worth nothing without the tapes, and those were all locked away somewhere. Not for trade. Property of this provisional government or that once everything on the old net was wiped.

"This is a Toshiba M-4-5-5," he said. "Are you out of your mind?"

I wasn't a shy girl. One of our hens had recently laid a half dozen eggs and, though it took about the same time as the others, one of those eggs was smaller and less bulbous, green as a cornstalk with ridges all around it.

"I've got an okra to trade," I said to him. The gathered crowd eclipsed me with their bickering, so I used my elbows to push towards the front.

He had a face hard to forget, pronounced jowls and a birthmark beside the bridge of his nose. He rang his little school bell – the one for announcing that someone had agreed to trade their okra. It took the crowd quieting down for my panic at the bell to subside. I hadn't even gotten Mamie's permission to tell anyone.

"Little girl, where's your okra?" he asked me.

I remembered Mamie screaming from the coop beside our trailer home and us thinking she was being attacked. Me and big Shan, we ran out. We found her in the coop and she's laughing like someone possessed by a demon.

"Shanti, you and your little sister come look at this…"

She was on her knees and stooped over it, elbows in the dirt. I'd never seen her like that.

The merchant hung his bell back on the rack and I came to my senses.

"Never mind," I said. He eyed me pensively. A moment passed when I thought about running.

"Your mamie's the one with the rooster show?" he asked. His lips were now arched in a smile and I couldn't tell whether to lie or tell the truth. I didn't challenge him taking my silence as a yes.

"Come inside and pick anything you want," he said. "Take it home and tell your mamie I'd like to pay y'all a visit."

The driver's name was Francois. *Francois Francois.* He was about twelve, sitting in that hot car all day like someone without any sense. He had a funny thing he told me he did, as a hobby. He said he studied the possibility of interdimensional emissions due to the blast. When I asked what he meant by that, he told me he would bring a telescope when they came to visit.

He was showing me items not on the display rack when our small talk progressed towards the festival in just a week. Then he asked a question I still think about from time to time.

"Why can't we just see them?"

*

We had many definitions for okra before the blast. The dictionary Mamie kept with the poetry book you got for your birthday calls it a plant.

Before the blast, okras came with seeds and you could plant them like apricots. To say you purchased one, you would also be acknowledging an earlier transaction. Pregnant seeds in fertile soil. Old things for new things. The thing with those okras is they met the same fate as avocados and coffee beans, and it all happened before the engine was built.

Francois said a laid okra defies natural law. Then he did the most surprising thing and told me not to trade Mamie's, whispered it in my ear while he showed me an old gaming console and the merchant visited the latrines nearby.

"Mamie says it might spoil," I whispered back. In my old age, I still recall the paranoia around owning one back then. Having it stolen was enough, before the imagined horror of pods losing their colour and the acrid whiff of decay spreading from the inside out.

"If what y'all have is an okra, your mamie has real reason to worry." Francois said this with enough conviction to make me believe.

"You talk like you're an expert," I told him. But it made sense. If it didn't come from earth as brown as the eyes beating down on me, it wasn't an okra. He called it extranormal, saying it resulted from a breakdown in causality. Francois and his pre-blast lexicon. School was once every week back then, and there was already too much to cram.

The console was a handheld. The screen had been cracked but Francois showed me it had some juice left. It had been retrofitted with a small solar panel and he advised me to take good care of it. On a scrap of paper, he scribbled the address for a repair shop that fixed pre-blast electronics.

I thanked him. We were at the big side door and he was getting ready to let me out when Mamie shouted my name. The door swung out and she was standing in front of the step rail, arms folded, face pinched in a frown.

The merchant still had his zipper down when he scurried up from behind her and spread his arms to block her entrance. When he was able to get a word out from under his breath, it spooked the birds that had congregated on the caravan's roof.

"Mamie Lennox, would you just listen?"

*

We ate the okra that night.

Better to blend it into a stew than trade it, Mamie had said. Or have it stolen from the cache under the trailer. Or watch it go bad.

Me and your namesake, we pleaded but she wouldn't hear it. She had Shan work the hand crank while she cut the okra into the other ingredients – tomatoes and peppers, palm oil and chicken broth once we had a fine paste.

Big Shan cried while she steered the crank. I came close to the blender and tears welled in my eyes next. My stomach growled at the smell, but the thought that I would never see Francois again forced a bitter taste into the stew.

The console kept me occupied till it was time to prepare for the festival.

*

A star is a sacred event. K.O. was adamant about this.

He had been beside himself when I told him we ate the okra. Years later. We went out for a walk by the old salt flat when talk of Mamie's hens came up.

She'd given them away before she passed. Big Shan went to live with a pen pal off the island and I was lost in too many reveries starring Francois. I wanted a new life, one without the coop or the smell that never washed off your hands. I wanted to travel. It's only funny years later that my first big rebellion after Mamie died led me to K.O.

"Babe, this water under your feet…" he said, "you should see how pretty it can get when there's a star."

"Ever seen one?"

"No, but I intend to— before I leave this realm for the next." He became wistful, his arm on my shoulders while he glanced off to where the flat vanished into the horizon and a half moon kept vigil on the island.

I was happy for the reprieve. He'd been teasing me for my alleged backwardness. This fanatical adherent to a system that originated before the blast and was now the domain of cultists convinced of the engine's mystic quality, offering it okras in the hope that it would grant them a glimpse of heaven in exchange.

Mamie only attended the festivals to show off her trick roosters.

K.O. returned to this realm and pulled me closer to his chest. "I'm thinking of raising a couple of hens myself," he said.

I pulled away, smacked him on the arm because I hated being ridiculed on top of everything else. "You're joking," I told him.

"Serious as a heart attack."

His eyes went wide as he spoke, telling me again why we were wrong to eat the okra.

The engine is without fault. It powered a ship that, had it not imploded on liftoff, would have ferried the tycoon who chartered it across the stars at a superluminal speed. The blast couldn't have been predicted. Nor could the war that followed. Nor the prior warnings about even attempting to build such an engine. It killed billions, and the war in its wake brought the world's population down to point two percent of what it had been. But the engine – fully constructed – signified victory over the old and oppressive laws of nature before the blast.

I listened. The blast cut off light from every star except our sun. I wasn't alive for it. Mamie heard firsthand accounts from people who protested the engine's construction, citing dangers too outlandish at the time to be taken seriously. She told me and big Shan she'd seen a star before we were born, and it wasn't during one of the festivals.

There'd been fighting – finger-pointing at first, then projectiles across the old borders. Who were the saboteurs behind the blast? The war took the power grids and the subsea cables and we came no closer to answering that.

Mamie was fourteen and travelling with a troupe that protested the fighting and brought animals on the road with them. The caravan had stopped for the night by an abandoned filling station. Mamie, finding everyone asleep, stepped outside to check on the trainer's twin elephant cubs. Orphans. Casualties from the war were almost double for those you could be sure had nothing to do with it.

There was a new moon. If Mamie couldn't tell by the usual absence over the horizon, she also described the feeling as fading into a shadow that stained the world like ink. She lit a match and trekked with her palm around the flame till she found the cubs in a clearing behind the station. They made trumpeting sounds in the dark while she shivered, watching the match go out.

She had the next match ready, but before she struck it, the sky flickered and she looked up.

Remembering what Francois had said about real okras, I turned, then sauntered playfully backwards with K.O. now face-to-face with me.

"What makes it an okra?" I asked.

"What do you mean?"

"Let's say you raise a hen that lays one, and you bring it to the festival this year. And the engine rewards the offering with a star—what do you do with the okra after you've seen the star?"

"Nothing," he said. "I don't care about no damn okras. I want to see a star. If I'm lucky, I'll get one as pretty as you."

"You think you're so smooth."

"Build a coop with me," he said.

I told him no. I don't recall if I meant it. The more okras accumulate in one place, the higher the chance of a star. I think people have just been hoarding their okras and pretending they were visited by one. That's what Mamie raised us to think.

*

I saw Francois again when I was fifteen. He came to a star festival. By then, it was me handling the roosters, and the old merchant had angered a cartel of poultry farmers who sunk their troubles down the big lake. Sometimes those troubles had a birthmark and a losing streak at the card tables, but that's somebody else's business, little Shan. Francois stole the caravan from him before all that, for all his time driving it and seeing nothing that resembled compensation.

There hadn't been a star that night. Dawn was almost breaking and the hopefuls had begun to disperse, okras going back where they kept them and the preservation rituals starting up again.

Big Shan was supposed to watch Mamie's roosters for me while I snuck off with Francois. We reached the top of the hill behind the market grounds and he must have re-parked that caravan a hundred times.

He'd spent a year off the island, some other part of the world where he got to be his age for a spell. He had the telescope welded to the old display rack. The merchant had traded every piece of it except the barrel and its peephole. Francois kept fussing about settings he couldn't adjust with what he had left, but eventually he found a place to park the caravan he was fine with.

The moon was a white swoop and the sky vantablack around it. He reminded me of the potted dracaena I kept by the window in our trailer, sprouting the way he did through his window, back arched, sinews on his dark brown skin as he flashed his yellow teeth and asked me to come back inside.

He pulled a small chair close to the telescope. I sat and he had me lean forward till the lens was on my right eye and my neck began to ache from how it was bent.

He asked me what I saw. Nothing at first. Nothing but the same darkness I'd seen since first looking up at night – darker than it ever got with my eyes closed. I didn't want to disappoint him, though, so I didn't answer.

"Don't take your eye off the scope," he said, like a voice in my head. My view through the lens had begun to stir a sense of foreboding in my chest and the instruction rattled me more than he probably intended.

He'd knelt beside the chair since I last looked at him. The view was still discomfiting when I went back to it. I blinked at the abyss through the lens. I let his baritone tuck itself in my ear, and my sense of everything around me crumbled.

"Before the blast, you could see Alpha Centauri at night, even without the scope. Alpha Centauri is a triple star system. A's just a little bigger than our sun. B's half as bright.

"Don't stop looking," he said when my elbow slipped from the armrest. "Normally, it only lasts a few seconds."

I adjusted my posture. The darkness turned a corner around me. I became weightless and unbound. Goosebumps pricked the skin under my button-up, the one Mamie had me wearing that night. She'd pressed it with the little strength she could still muster and handed me a pristine pair of gloves to match.

I waited a long time for that first glimpse. It started with the faintest flash of light, then clouds that swelled into oblongs and blurred slowly in and out. One cloud was brighter than the other, but they both looked like mist, like smoke from the collector's pipe.

Something flickered in the middle of each cloud and sparked a memory I didn't know I had, memory of that precise moment. Two floating points of light – and perhaps I'd been one of them.

It felt like a reunion. I knew I was imagining this connection but that's how most things begin, little Shan. Everything you're meant to understand in this life will feel like a memory you had to unlock first. And I understood. The name for what I felt stayed hidden from me, but I understood.

I turned, and the image followed after me. "Francois," I whispered. One of the stars winked. The other wouldn't stop radiating. It blossomed into a white smudge across my vision field, then everything faded out.

I felt my weight again. I felt the ache in my neck. My eyes grew heavy and, remembering it was almost dawn, I pulled away from the telescope.

I didn't want to lose the after-image, so I shut my eyes. It must have taken less time than it felt to burn out, and if Francois said anything to me while I waited, I couldn't hear it. I breathed.

"That was lovely," I told him.

He hadn't moved from where he knelt in the corner of my eye. "That's the engine's grace," he replied.

He said it like the priest who used to live next door would say it later on, when K.O. would invite himself over and drag me along.

"Tell me what you actually think it is," I said to him. I'd never been more curious about it than I was all of a sudden. When you grow up not seeing the night sky, it can be hard to know what you've missed. "Why can't we see them like we used to?"

He told me before the blast, everything had an order to which it adhered, and all previous engines were no exception. Something happened with this one that caused a breakdown in causality – a rupture or some other strain on the system.

"A lot of people are trying to figure out what," he said. "A few here on the island."

By then, I'd done a little more schooling and had an idea what he meant. All the old laws of nature had to be reargued after the blast. It's what I was taught and, if I could guess, it's what they're teaching you now.

I don't know why we can't just see them. I sat in that caravan and I absorbed everything he said like I had a quiz on it the next morning. I studied at the college he talked about wanting to attend. I never learned how to describe what seeing the two he showed me made me feel, but if there's one thing I now know with complete certainty, it's that I want it for me. I want it for all of us.

Francois scooted closer and stared like he wanted to laugh. "Would that be worth your mamie's okra?" he asked.

"Worth more," I said.

His eyes twitched as I looked down at them. He smiled flatly at me and said he had to be getting back. We kissed.

We were gone for a week. We took the causeway across the big lake, and it only bothered me a little how much trouble I'd be in when I got home to Mamie and Shan.

We lodged with a member of his kite-building club – that had become his trade since cutting ties with the merchant. She peppered me with questions about Mamie's okra. I didn't have it in me to say what we'd done with it, so I was happy when Francois changed the subject.

It's funny thinking about it now. He'd only brought up the okra once up to that point, and continued to act uninterested the whole week. Maybe he knew. Maybe he thought I would lie to him, pretend a star had shone on us and taken the okra as gratuity. Truthfully I didn't know him too well, and never got the chance, but I could sense his exhaustion with that period in his life, and his desire to move on.

I lost him around the time we lost Mamie. Her condition progressed past the point where anything could be done. She'd found someone from the old troupe to care for her roosters and no longer hated me for losing one of them. She even grew to like Francois. That merchant just had to be out of the picture first.

We were going to elope. One morning, they found the caravan under the big lake, but no Francois.

*

With this year's festival approaching, I've been asked to bring K.O.'s okra again. I never hesitate when I do. It's what K.O. would've wanted, and while he's no longer here with us, his wish to see a star before he died now consumes me. As if it's mine.

Before leaving for the festival, I first inspect the wrap around the okra. I don't know why I put it in a wrap, except to please the collector. Remember, little Shan, okras don't spoil.

The collector wheels out his crates from the back of his rover. The okras inside them look less like they should each year. He insists it's how they look when properly preserved, making his rounds, finding others at the festival who don't know better and convincing them to inject his homemade poison into theirs.

As early as noon, we've already begun to convene on the market grounds. Priests and poultry farmers. Musicians, artisans, politickers and so on. We congregate underneath canopies normally reserved for bartering and while the afternoon away with music from antiquated instruments or stories of sightings elsewhere on the island. When I'm asked to share mine, I don't include what led to it or what came after. It's often still difficult to talk about. The collector claims, for this reason, K.O.'s okra – my okra – is worth more than the others at the festival.

One of these days, I'll just eat the damn thing.

I saw two stars in my lifetime and there were no okras nearby. When I go to sleep now I see constellations. I see heaven and I see a way there. A ship with enough room for all of us. For this and all future generations. You and your mamie. K.O. Francois.

We'll have our reunion in the realm where the stars went. We'll build a new engine to get us there. Though only a dream for now – only a memory of nonexistent good things, this engine we build will power a ship as big and boundless as you can conceive, little Shan. It won't be without fault. It won't be completed quickly enough for everyone, but its construction will not be driven by the solipsist whims of a tycoon or captain of industry.

Do you dream of such an engine?

Obstructive Nodes – The Etiquette of Complaint – A Pest Problem

Adrian Tchaikovsky

B-991 was at it again.

V-330 looked at the new slip with disgust. Oh, the text was there, waiting to be transliterated. He could do his job. And yet there was the rest. The writing around the borders. Lower case, untidy.

V-330 was the designation of the node, of course. He could remember, a long time ago when he had been younger, when people had called him Yori. Yori was not a node name, though. Since taking up his position, here in the tight confines of V-330, then that was what the world knew him as. He had tried, in the brief periods he had between finishing shift and sleep claiming him, to internalise this. *I am V-330.* It would, he was sure, make him a more efficient worker, and ensure that his small part of the great task was completed with a greater efficiency. To his shame, those youthful memories would not recede into final oblivion. In his head he remained Yori.

But that didn't mean that he was going to think of B-991 as Venya.

That had been how it had started. The slip had come through, reading as follows:

SJGW-FD-JWKK-PGLA-LLAHFJW-MMSHF
SNF-NQWJHVLO-NZJP-A-FNDO-FSSF-SAF
HJDK-KKAAS-NJWSC-ANV-EWRFR-TITS

And, below the prescribed characters for Yori to transliterate, was a little scribble. Joined-up, messy writing unlike the blocky characters of the message's text. *Tits. Sounds rude! I'm Venya. What's your name?*

The operative in node B-991 was not *Venya*. They were B-991. That was how it worked. Yori had ignored the ridiculous, inefficient rider and set to work. His node, as all nodes, came with a whole shelf of enormous cypher books, and he'd identified the correct volumes covering the alphabet or character set of the message that B-991 had passed him. Painstakingly, yet as swiftly as possible, he'd looked up each character, noted down the corresponding symbol – in another character set entirely, usually – that it should be recorded as, and quickly filled out his own little slip with the appropriately encoded message, which he passed through the slot downstream to G-081. In Yori's outputted version, the final four characters had not read TITS or anything that might – by someone less professional – be considered amusing. And while Yori'd had the opportunity to add some personal message to G-081, strictly against protocol, he did not. What was he going to say, anyway? *B-991 thought this was funny but it's not now. B-991 is Venya. Hi, I'm Yori, who are you?* Stupidity.

In asking Yori his own name, B-991 had also displayed a staggering ignorance of how the nodes worked. The message slips only went one way. Yori's node had five slots feeding in to him, and one slot feeding out to G-081. Yes, it would have been theoretically possible for him to scrawl something on B-991's own used slip and force-feed it back through the slot, but that was quite improper. When they collected his bin of used slips, probably they'd notice he had one too few, and his neighbour one too many. It would mean a reprimand, at the very least. It would show that he, Yori, V-330, was not taking his work seriously. His domain, V-330, was a vital hub in the very important activity of the transliteration process. He was being trusted with a great level of responsibility. If he started messing around, who knew what could happen? He might fall below some level of efficiency set up within the system, and be disciplined. He might incorrectly translate a character, meaning that the message he passed downstream to G-081 – and every stage of the process from G-081 onwards – would be *wrong*. He shuddered at the very thought.

And yet here was B-991, doodling and writing and spending valuable *time* when there was work to be done.

Ever since that first time, every slip Yori received through the slot that linked his node to B-991 had contained some sort of personalised addition. At first it had been little notes like the first, asking him about himself, telling him things about B-991 – *Venya* – he hadn't wanted to know. And, because he'd trained himself rigorously to scan every character on the slips, Yori hadn't been able to stop himself reading all of that nonsense. Which meant that his valuable time was being wasted in non-work-related activity, compromising his efficiency. It was all very well that B-991 appeared to be able to send slips in to Yori just as quickly as the other four input slots leading into V-330, as *well* as annotate them with these unprofessional scribbles. Yori, being downstream, had a busier schedule than those *flaneurs* one step earlier in the process. Busier by *five*, in fact. He couldn't be expected to waste time reading letters and words that weren't to be transliterated. And yet his eyes were hauled through every new and unapproved addition like a man being dragged through barbed wire.

Just little pleasantries, at first, but then B-991 had become creative. There had been doodles. Weird, wonky amateurish scribbles of sheep and birds and gurning human faces. That had been bad enough. And now verse. The most recent slip had the following, spiralling around its periphery, surrounding the approved text like raiders creeping in from all sides:

> The thronging pens of bards and poets carve
> Romance replete with all those folk whose knell
> Was 'One who loved not wisely but too well'
> And praise heroic souls who died for love
> While by their own hands slain.
> No thought is spent on those who merely
> Sighed and tried again.

And that was precisely four and a half seconds of Yori's busy working day that he wouldn't be getting back.

His schedule bell sounded then, and he obediently stopped work to eat. This was officially 'personal time', but if he didn't eat the paper-wrapped packet of grey paste sandwiches they'd provided for him now, there wouldn't be another chance. He could hardly send G-081, that hardworking node, transliterated slips smudged with grease. The fingerprints of Yori, V-330, recorded on them as though he, too, was trying to get his downstream neighbour interested in him as a *person*! Wholly inappropriate.

If he absolutely bolted the sandwiches he could technically spend the rest of his personal time any way that he chose. He could sit and stare at this wall of his node, or at that one. At the ceiling, even, should he feel the need for a change of view. He could, if he had been so unprofessional, write bad verse on some of the blank slips. Maybe B-991 was just a really fast eater, and that was how they did it.

Another thing he could theoretically do would be to contact his supervisor. There was a funnel, for that. Not just a slot, a rectangle of not-wall giving onto a neighbouring node. A funnel that allowed a written note to be carried, by the modern principles of electric suction, to some unguessable place where, Yori was informed, there was a supervisor.

If Yori was five times as busy as B-991, and G-081 was presumably five times as busy as Yori, the thought of how busy their *supervisor* must be brought him out in sweats. To be responsible for all the nodes, however many that might be. Or even just for a section of nodes. Even just a handful. The supervisor must be constantly attending to matters of the utmost importance. They must have no personal time for themselves at all. They must have developed some method of sandwich consumption that practically defied the principles of physics, in order to make time for the throng of important matters that doubtless occupied their time. The sheer thought of such an august personage, on whose shoulders so much weight must be balanced, was enough to make a poor node operative tremble. And yet...

And yet Yori sat here, dutiful, diligent, and felt his own work efficiency erode in the face of a constant stream of irrelevant marginalia from B-991. From *Venya*. No, from B-991, and now he'd spent a whole two extra seconds fussing over the proper designation of his unruly neighbour. Two seconds he owed to his *job*. That was like theft. B-991 had stolen from him, and from their mutual employer.

He bolted the last crumbs of his sandwich and brought out the report slip.

He had been writing it over many days now, adding a handful of words in the last slivers of each period of personal time. Even doing this made Yori feel guilty. Even though it was nothing compared to B-991's relentless onslaught of nonsense. Even though it was entirely devoted towards restoring proper workplace efficiency.

By now the message he'd been piecing together in his free seconds was almost complete. It read:

To the esteemed supervisor

I wish to raise a complaint concerning my upstream neighbour Node B-991. Slips received from that direction are reaching me embroidered with unnecessary non-work text that negatively impacts my own ability to perform my job. I estimate that as many as eighty seconds per shift are being lost in needless distraction owing to this unauthorised communication. I would ask that appropriate sanctions and measures are put in place to prevent B-991 imposing on their fellow workers in such an untoward and intrusive manner.

With only a few seconds to go before his shift recommenced, he almost committed a cardinal sin by writing *Yori* at the foot of the slip, which would have been unforgivable. Recalling himself just in time, he wrote *V-330* and then had precisely one spare second in which to stare down at the completed message before his schedule rang to inform him he should get back to work.

The report slip sat at Yori's elbow for the rest of his shift. Although his desk space was small, and mostly occluded by the open pages of whichever encryption manual he was working from, he avoided so much as brushing the slightly curled rectangle of thin paper. As though, in his mind, it was red hot, and even the slightest contact would leave a permanent mark. It was a new thing in his world. It was a complaint.

Admittedly, he had complained before. Months ago, he had heard the occupant of F-118, to his right, snoring. It had come every day. Possibly it had been in F-118's personal time but, if so, F-118 had been allowed considerably more personal time than Yori. The snoring had been vexing, but honestly it had been that other thought which had driven him to write his report. The idea that this person, who probably had a far less important job than he by a factor of five, received a greater allocation of personal time. Where was the justice? And so he had written a complaint, with great trepidation. He had fed it into the mouth of the supervisor's hose and it had been vacuumed away at great expense. And, a day later, the snoring had stopped, and the rate of messages from F-118 had increased markedly. And while that technically meant that Yori's own workload was that much greater, he felt a profound inner satisfaction at having improved the system as a whole and ensured the occupant of F-118 was not slacking or skiving or having a better time than Yori.

It was possible that B-991 also had a greater allocation of personal time than Yori did, and that they were writing their poems and drawing their sketches in this permitted lacuna. This did not mean, surely, that they were entitled to inflict doggerel onto poor hardworking colleagues whose work was sufficiently important that they had no free time of their own.

It was also possible that B-991 was *not* the originator of the little notes, but that they were faithfully either copying or transliterating unauthorised text they had received from upstream. That thought had occurred to Yori a while back, and frozen him with terror for almost thirteen valuable seconds. What if *Yori* was also supposed to be doing the same, just transliterating the marginalia for G-081. What if, instead of being diligent, he had been introducing errors into the system.

That had earned him a sleep period where he'd lain awake, frantically going through the logic of the situation, horrified at the possibility he'd committed so gross an error. By the end of that three-hour period though, he had restored an inner equilibrium. No other node's data included the aberrant additions that B-991's did, and the format of the extra text did not match the clear characters that Yori spent his day looking up in the books and then translating for G-081. This was a jolly of B-991's own. This was someone playing a joke on poor hardworking Yori.

And still he didn't send the report, not even when his schedule told him his shift had ended and he should immediately go to sleep to gain the maximum amount of recuperation before the next one began in three hours. He had not slept well, after F-118. Consciously, of course, he had been delighted. The snoring bastard was gone, efficiency was increased. Yori – though slightly more overworked – could bask in the satisfaction of having dutifully made the world a better place. And yet some subconscious part of him had twisted uncomfortably. He didn't wonder where F-118 had gone, obviously. F-118 was still there. It was the node. The occupant wasn't really important. And the new occupant had the sort of mechanical efficiency that Yori envied, honestly. The slips came through far more reliably and rapidly than ever the snorer had managed. But some part of him could not escape the fact that *something* was gone from the world, and that he was the root cause of its subtraction.

The next day, though, a slip came through B-991's slot that was too much. An offence. An assault, honestly, on the entire system. As though B-991 was well aware that Yori had been teetering on the brink of filing a report and had decided to deliberately push him over. Yes, pure malice was what it was. No other explanation was possible.

Around the edges of the slip, enclosing the honest, blocky characters of the proper message, was the following:

Do you ever stop to wonder what any of these mean?
Whether they ever had a meaning at the start?
Whether there even is a start to this process?
Or if the same messages are just going round and round?

The insidious suggestion made Yori's hands shake as he noted down the translations. B-991 had crossed from frivolous to actively seditious. Yes, it was true that the messages on the slips meant nothing to Yori, but they weren't *supposed* to. That was above his pay grade. Obviously there was a point in the system where the messages came in, meaning something. Then each node in turn took them, looked the characters up in the appropriate manual, transliterated them into the appropriate characters in a new alphabet or symbol array or set of characters, and delivered them to the next node downstream. Where someone like Yori would go through the same process and pass them on. And eventually they would get where they were going. And fulfil their purpose. They would be decoded and read. The plan would be advanced. Somewhere down there was someone who was working five or twenty-five or 125 or 625 times as hard as Yori, and they were the point of all this effort, and they were utterly dependant on Yori doing his job. A job that was in danger because his head was full of the nonsense sent to him by B-991.

Obviously they couldn't just be passing the same messages round and round from node to node. It was true that it *could* work like that. After another node had got hold of a message and transliterated it, there was no way that Yori would have been able to recognise it. Not after it had passed through a couple of other alphabets or character sets. And it was true that, logistically, a circular system would actually be easier to set up than one funnelling from so many, down to some singular exit point. A system where everyone just passed everything round, rather than the hierarchy of work that would require someone three steps beyond Yori to be working over a thousand times as hard to process all the messages. Yes, logistically, that would be entirely possible, but it would make a mockery of the entire business. Why, instead of very important work for a vital system, Yori's life might almost be meaningless. Not even a cog in a great machine, but just a flywheel spinning with great energy but to no noticeable effect.

This last message from B-991 was the final straw. When his schedule sounded the advent of his personal time he bolted his grey sandwich and fed his report into the supervisor's duct almost vengefully.

The next shift, the slips that fed in from B-991 were clear of distractions. Just the simple, plain message for Yori to transliterate. No doodles, no poems, no destabilizing suggestions about the work. Just efficiency. Obviously an improvement.

He did not, under any circumstances, find himself missing the notes, the jokes, the rhymes. That would be entirely the opposite of how he felt about the business. He could just get on with his work in peace and without having to think in unprofessional ways.

The new occupant of B-991 was more efficient, just as the new F-118 had been. Yori had to increase his own productivity just to keep up. It made him proud, obviously. He had helped the system. He had even forced himself to push his own limits, become a better worker. Now all five of his neighbours were feeding slips to him almost non-stop, and he was frantically ripping manuals from the shelves, running his fingers down the dense text, and writing his own slips, which he shoved into the slot to G-081.

At one point – he wasn't sure of this, because the pace he was working meant he was really very tired all the time – he thought that G-081 had been trying to shove a slip back up into his node. Obviously that wasn't how it worked. Obviously he was mistaken. Or else G-081 had made an error. Obviously he hadn't seen, written on the back of that intruding piece of filmy paper, the words *Slow down! Can't keep up!* before his own slip shoved it back down and out of sight. Because if G-081 had really been so short of time then they wouldn't have had the chance to be standing on their chair trying to shove a handwritten note back up the chain, would they? It only stood to reason.

Some shifts later there was another personal message. Seeing it, Yori's heart leapt. Or sank, obviously. Sank was definitely the proper word. Leapt would be wholly inappropriate. It came on a slip from K-243, a node on Yori's left that had only ever been professional in all the time he'd been at work. Just the proper messages, delivered with speed and efficiency and in nice neat writing. A pleasure to work with, a real credit to the organisation. But now this, written in a shaky hand along the very bottom edge of the slip.

Are you still you? I'm still me. Am I the last one left?

At least K-243 wasn't insisting on having a *name* or anything, but the content of the message was still disquieting. Yori didn't know what to make of it. It didn't have the playfulness of B-991's timewasting. It seemed to be expressing something important in an alphabet that Yori didn't have the manual for.

In his free time, after practically swallowing his sandwich in a single gulp, he actually got as far as writing a reply. The fact horrified him. He must be very tired to even consider it. Obviously he wouldn't be trying to shove the slip *upstream* into K-243's slot. That would be wholly unprofessional.

At the end of the shift he looked at the slip, incriminating, sitting on his desk.

I'm me. I'm Yori. I'm here.

Meaningless. Just words. To send such nonsense anywhere would be to sneer at the great and rigorous system they were all a part of. To spit on their important work.

He didn't even dare put the slip in the bin, because probably there were other workers going through everyone's used slips, to make sure that this sort of timewasting wasn't going on. And while they hadn't taken any action against the egregious B-991 until Yori himself had written a complaint, that didn't mean that his own aberrant behaviour wouldn't be picked up. In the end he ate the slip, not unlike the sandwiches in general taste and constitution. Yes, he would be one slip light, should they audit him for that, but easier to explain that than his stupid little message.

K-243 did not try to communicate again. Instead, they obviously regretted the lapse and applied themselves to their own work all the more diligently, because their slip output increased noticeably, so that Yori had to up his own pace yet again. Which meant, he told himself, that the system was working better.

Life, if you could call it living, went on like this. And yet somehow Yori found himself looking at each slip fed through the slot from B-991. As though he might see a drawing there, or a note, or a rhyming couplet. There was nothing but the approved text, of course, in characters infinitely clear and unvarying. Just as it should be.

He had put all of B-991's annotated slips into the bin. Of course. He found himself wishing that he had kept some. Just a few of them. Even just one. Which would have been impermissible, plainly, but he could have slipped it in between the pages of one of the manuals and it seemed unlikely anyone would have found it. There had never been a search or inspection of his node, after all.

In all honesty he wasn't entirely sure how anyone would have been able to get in to perform such a function.

One shift, soon after that single odd communication from K-243, Yori felt himself gripped by a feeling he could neither understand nor master. He had just finished transliterating a slip from F-118, but instead of shoving it straight down into G-081 as he should, he found himself just staring down at it.

This means nothing to me, he thought. And of course it didn't. Neither in the original he had received, nor in the version he was about to dispatch. It wasn't supposed to mean anything to him. Interpretation wasn't his function. He was just…

A transliterator. A very important node in the system of… The System. Why, if he didn't do his job with peak efficiency then… anything might happen. Chaos.

He took up the slip from F-118 with its original, incomprehensible text.

He wrote on it.

I'm Yori. Who are you?

He didn't have a rude icebreaker joke he could make, at the expense of the message.

He sent his proper translation down to G-081, as he was supposed to. Then he leant over to the slot through to B-991. Another slip was feeding through, and he pulled it out almost impatiently. Then, before the productive worker in the neighbouring cubicle could start on a new one, he shoved his own message through, crumpling and creasing it as he forced it the wrong way up the chain.

He sat down, feeling his heart hammer. Knowing he'd done a terrible thing. Waiting for them to come and get him for disciplinary purposes.

Although, now he thought about it, he wasn't really sure how they'd do that.

He worked for the rest of the day. Nothing bad happened. It was just the work. When his schedule sounded, he broke for personal time. The sandwiches were the same too.

The first slip from B-991, after his break, had something extra written on it.

He stared at it. He didn't really understand. The writing was that exact same neat script, but in an extra line to one side, crunched into the margin.

We are ants.

It seemed a strange thing to write. A philosophical point, presumably. A metaphor. Ants were efficient and loyal workers, after all. They were proverbial for their industry, unless that was bees. But bees and ants were, in any event, closely related, and so the point stood. Yori considered this. Perhaps from a certain point of view the workers in the nodes *were* all ants. All of them. Conscientious and diligent workers for the greater good.

The next shift he fed a message to F-118, thrilling at his own daring.

I am Yori. Who are you? B-991 says we are ants.

Not long after, one of the slips from F-118 came with another little margin note, in that obsessively regular script.

Yes we are ants.

Yori thrilled. A dialogue had begun. An exchange of ideas. Ideas in support of the system, so not seditious, surely. Probably he was inspiring his neighbours to greater heights of efficiency. Over the next few days, he communicated this idea to the other nodes around him and was delighted to find that they were all of a mind concerning the ant-like nature of their role. They were neither condemnatory nor congratulatory in respect of this, simply restating the observation as though it were fact. After a few days, Yori found himself a little frustrated that none of his neighbours was willing to take the intellectual lead in their new school of thought. Nobody developed the idea, or even showed any sign that there was anything more to say. He began to write little notes in the edges of his personal time, trying to provoke a more edifying response.

In what way could we be more like ants?

What are the chief virtues of being like ants?

Is a Queen Ant the originator or recipient of our messages?

But none of his neighbouring nodes contributed anything more than a repetition that they were, indeed, ants. The philosophy had proved unexpectedly reductive. This late flowering of thought, which Yori had initially been inspired by, had become stagnant very rapidly. The development frustrated him. His messages shifted into the provocative, just to try and get his colleagues to think properly about the merits of their situation.

Are we just ants?

Can we not be more than ants?

What's so great about ants?

Those few replies he received suggested his neighbours didn't even understand what he was trying to say:

We are ants.

We are only ants.

We are all ants.

By now Yori was aware that his own efficiency had been compromised, and he was sending out dozens of extra messages a day. Anyone auditing him would note that his stock of blank slips was decreasing far faster than his actual output to G-081 could account for. And yet the intractability of his fellows incensed him. *Am I the only one around here who actually thinks?* he raged inwardly.

He was working on a manifesto. Or, as he called it *The Antifesto*, because there was nothing of humanity in it. Writing on spare slips that should have gone into the bin, numbering them as best he could to keep them ordered. A diatribe on the place of the individual within the system. Not seditious at all, obviously. Just Yori, V-330, doing his best for the greater good, because surely if he could understand his role within the whole then he would be a better worker for it.

There was a *shthunk!* noise.

Yori stopped writing. The background noise to his life was the constant whisper of slips feeding through slots. That was how things should be. Nothing had ever gone *shthunk!* before.

It was a long and inefficient few minutes of wasted work time before he found where the sound had come from. It was the hose leading to his supervisor, a thing he'd barely thought about for many shifts. It had *delivered* a message to him. He had no idea that its pneumatic system even worked two ways. Certainly none of his past reports had ever been acknowledged, save by the replacement of his annoying neighbours.

He took the slip with trembling hands. Perhaps his superiors had noticed his promise in the field of work-related philosophy.

It read:

A complaint has been received regarding your efficiency.

Yori read it again, and a third time. The wording didn't change, although he was certainly tired enough to have misread it on the first outing.

It was true that the incoming slips had piled up somewhat, because of his philosophical debates with his neighbours and *The Antifesto* and all. But this was an outrage! He, the system's most devoted son, the Antiest of the Ants, dedicated to not only doing his job but justifying it in terms impossible to argue against!

He stood up, there in his node. He banged on the wall to B-991.

"Hey!" he said. "Can you believe this? They say someone's complained!"

There was no response from B-991. No great surprise, because Yori's croak was the first human voice he'd heard in… well, as long as he could recall maybe. Certainly since he'd stopped being Yori and become V-330. But still, these were exceptional circumstances! He was insulted. He was traduced!

"Hey!" he shouted again, and put his eye right up against the slot. He wanted to see the bastard. Probably it was B-991 who'd complained, dragged Yori's good name – or at least his good number – through the mud.

After he'd seen what there was to see, he sat down behind his desk again. Stared at the pen. Stared at the manuals. Stared at the slips as they fed in one after another from all sides.

A bustle of industry, was what he'd seen. Diligent and hardworking and in constant motion. Probably they didn't even get personal time, his neighbours. The constant seethe and flurry of them, their trembling antennae, the bustling of their tiny segmented bodies.

For the second time ever, in his professional career, he heard *Shthunk!*

He sat there a little while before reaching over and plucking the rolled-up message from the hose. Right then, there didn't seem to be any urgency. Flattening it out, his eyes passed almost disinterestedly across the text.

For reasons of reorganisation and productivity you are being replaced.

Yori nodded. He'd thought it would be something like that. He thought about B-991. The previous one, the one who'd written little verses and drawn cartoon animals. The one he'd complained about.

"Well," he told the walls of his node, "good luck to them getting me out of here. There's no door."

Only when the skittering host of bodies began to force their way in through the slots did he understand.

The Earth Heals – Silent Days – Vagaries and Savagery

Anne Charnock

I send my team ahead of me to the monthly gathering – a forty-minute trek through the forest and a half-hour stroll across grasslands – while I don my jacket and turn on the rain. It's a rare, rare moment to have the forest to myself. I peer out, rain pattering on my hood: a riot of hazel, birch and sessile oak. Emerald epiphytes colonise every tree, every boulder and rotting stump. Miniature polypody ferns litter the moss-covered branches and colonise the tiniest nooks wherever rainwater collects. I'm alone, but not *alone*. A male redstart flits from an oak branch to the undulating, verdant forest floor, gorging itself on insects living within these swelling, prodigious waves of mosses, liverworts and lichens. I turn three-sixty degrees: there is no exposed bark whatsoever. No bare rock. A gorgeous, soaking burgeoning of life.

I take a deep breath knowing these trees are giving me oxygen, giving me life. And I release my breath knowing I am, in turn, bringing life to the trees and all the greenery that befriends them. It all makes sense. Everything makes sense here. We will achieve our goal through our children and grandchildren, and ever onwards, as we have held true all these years, building on the endeavours of our antecedents. One thousand acres for one thousand years. We will preserve our temperate ecosystems for the future, hoping, trusting, that our withered world – *the outside* – will one day be healed. But whenever I look out beyond the glass panels of our biospheres, I wonder what sight exactly would tempt everyone to decamp, to leave our glassy domes, the only home we have known?

The redstart reappears – fiery red breast and red tail, black face and black throat – popping out from a tree cavity in one of our oldest oaks. Does he realise he lives within a biosphere, that his freedom is constrained, that he cannot migrate?

I clamber through the rainforest and stride out across the grasslands feeling energised and light. The summer meadows always have this effect on me. Everything seems possible. But I pull up at the sight of a small bird perching perilously on a tall stalk of grass. A male wood warbler has somehow escaped the rainforest. What are you doing here, little fella? I shake with laughter. He'll be okay, I suppose, because all our biospheres are temperate: rainforest, grassland, lake and sea loch. Maybe the warbler will remember his way back.

As I set off again, mindful of the time, I thank the ancestors who battled through the centuries to keep their precious biomes alive, dealing with one near-collapse after another. These summer meadows are surely their sweetest benefaction.

I count my steps. I'm attempting to calm myself before the gathering. It's time I spoke my mind, but I need to be persuasive. So, I commit to memory a string of single words and prompts: *timidity, contented, look outward instead of inward, those space colonists*. I rehearse my arguments, summon phrases that will spear, convince: *Feel the wind blow! Don't you dream?* I could begin: *A healthy community is a happy community.* Too vague? Our leader, Bala, would probably cut me off. I can almost hear her voice: *No, no,* no. *This is not a subject for the gathering. Why are you so flighty? Try to be more practical.*

Leaving the grasslands, I enter home-farm. One of the poultry workers, Jackson, raises his hand and calls out. "The earth heals."

I reply, "With our love and care."

"Wait for me." He throws off his apron.

I like to hang out with the home-farmers, and I've spent more than my share of Wednesday and Sunday evenings with Jackson, come to think of it. See, the mood around home-farmers tends to be lighthearted. They have such a reputation for silliness and pranks. I think it's working with hens and chicks, goats and kids, that does it. Being around all that playful, often nonsensical innocence.

"You look unusually flustered," I say.

"I've cleaned two henhouses this morning. I've two more to clean after the gathering."

"Can't you leave them for tomorrow?"

"Well, you tree-folk don't understand." He nudges me, shoulder to shoulder, and laughs. "In the wilds, you can let things run their course, can't you?" I start to protest but give way. "With hens and goats, there's no end of grief: diseases, infections. If it's not one thing it's another. So, no, I won't put off cleaning the henhouses. I couldn't face another cull. And you'll be the first to complain if eggs and chicken are off the menu for six months." He brushes down his clothes with his hands. "And that's not all. One of my hens is being henpecked something awful, and I can't get a beak guard on the culprit. I think my hands are too big."

"I could do it. I'll come by later if you like."

"Oh, no need. I'll put her in a separate coop to recover."

"Shouldn't the culprit be separated out."

He guffaws. "Gods alive! They're chickens! Not humans." I speed up to keep pace with him. "I suppose you'll have something to say at the gathering. You usually do."

I shrug, refuse an answer. We pass the rows of pole beans and aubergines, skirt around the vertical farming racks. As we near the grassed amphitheatre, we join the end of the queue and sit just below the top rim.

Bala has started her preamble and waves impatiently to the latecomers, encouraging us to take our places. Before everyone is finally settled, she announces the first item on the agenda – home-farm yields. She always rushes our discussions, I feel, with no one allowed to ramble, whoever they are and whatever their age. Every gathering is guillotined when she states, baldly, "We all have work to do!"

I realise I'm clenching and unclenching my fists, so I place my palms flat on my knees. Should I wait until it's my turn to be leader?

It would be far easier to effect change if I held the main voice, if I set the agenda. My name could be pulled out next month, or I could be waiting years from now. Our lottery has proved to be fair – and though some people are not really cut out for the job, there's a limit to how much damage they can do in two years. But to my mind, a run of cautious leaders has been detrimental, and I can't be the only one who is chafing.

Tree thinning is the second item on the agenda which is contentious as several seniors have chuntered ahead of this gathering that we thinned and coppiced the rainforest too much last year. The elders are always at it, trying to assert themselves, but they should restrict their carping to the old-timers' coffee haunts. Jackson turns and stares at me, as though expecting me to speak. I'm saving myself. Instead, another worker from our biosphere, raises a hand and interjects. "It's true, we've seen a fall off in total biomass, specifically in insect biomass after the thinning. It's a delicate balance – woodland versus open glades. Both are important." He's about to sit down, but decides to add, "In any case, we all accept that it's beneficial to shock our ecosystems from time to time. Speaking for our own sphere, we need to keep checking the resilience of our biome." I stand and clap enthusiastically. Others follow. When we settle back into our seats, Jackson jumps up. "It's the same on home-farm. We stress our crops periodically. It's nature's way. We need to know that one day when we migrate outdoors, that our crops and animals will be resilient, whatever our Mother throws at us." Bala wraps up the discussion by announcing she will visit the rainforest herself and report back at the next gathering. I see her shoulders relax, evidently relieved she has nipped things in the bud.

Next. A report from our medical officer. This could be my chance. He states that the overall health of our community has improved over the past six months, with a small but significant weight gain across all age groups. Fungal issues are lessening but he reminds everyone to take all precautions. He reports one serious injury, a leg break, though the patient is on the mend and should be back at work in a month's time on light duties. Overall levels of contentedness are currently satisfactory.

He invites any questions.

I leap up, place a hand on my chest, take a deep breath. "How lucky are we that our ancestors were chosen to live and work here?" I cast glances and note the nods of agreement. "They chose Earth. They did not take flight, as they might have done. Surely many had the opportunity as scientists and specialists of one type or another." Bala holds out her hands as if to ask where the hell this might be going. Undeterred: "And we hear that the colonists are making the same old mistakes as though their host planets deserve no respect." I pause, steeling myself. "Yet we live here, timid, cowering, *merely contented*, afraid of the outside world. You may not see it that way, you may not feel timid. *Contented* may be enough for many of you, and I respect that. But I ask you all, is our life here so different to the lives of those space colonists? We stick to our domes. The colonists cannot venture out unaided – imagine that – but we could walk outside right now without a stitch of clothing."

A ripple of laughter is brought to a halt by Bala. "What is your actual point? Time presses."

"I would be happier, as opposed to *contented*, if we could venture out more often and for longer, not simply to take samples and maintain our weather stations. I imagine that some of you here have not ventured out in years. My point is this: we must form a study group to set a timeline for migrating outdoors. After all, patches of greenery have been spotted from our farthest weather station. Surely it is safe now for the children to have an occasional lesson outdoors, to witness and explore our reality. Just as man saw Earth from space for the first time, our children must see this world from the outside."

An elder sitting low down in the amphitheatre pulls himself off the grass with some effort and looks up at me, pointing. "You are always wanting more, aren't you? Why take the risk? We don't know it's safe to spend an extended period of time outside."

"I'd volunteer to find out!" I take a deep breath. I won't let him rile me. He won't be able to speak at gatherings for much longer. He's almost fifty. I point at him. "It is my right at my age to speak my mind. Whereas you will enter your silent days soon. Is it next year? We will be obliged to manage without your quips at our gatherings." Which raises open laughter. He sits back down, and for a moment I feel shame for the hurt I may have caused. I call out. "Forgive me, if you have taken any offence." But I can't let him undermine me, so I press on, holding out my open palm towards him. "You must yield to us younger ones. It's our right to be heard first and foremost. Didn't the elders cause all our problems in the first place? And understand this: I speak for our future, for our one big dream to be realised. We need to feel the future is near."

"No, that's enough," shouts the leader. "You must learn patience. It's the safest way."

I climb past my neighbours and stride down towards the centre of the amphitheatre. I march straight to our boulder, "I claim my right to speak." I place my palm on the boulder, and the gathering settles. "I claim my right. I ask you to think on this: surely you will agree. We need to re-acclimatise, slowly. Spend a little more time out there and get accustomed to the vagaries – and yes! the savagery – of the outside world. The longer we wait, the more difficult it will be." There is little point saying more, but before I withdraw, I call out, exasperated, "Don't you want to stand outside? Outside! And feel the wind blow from pole to pole?"

In the cacophony, it's difficult to judge if I've won people over.

*

"Well, you ruffled feathers! Why the drama?"

Trust a poultry worker to make light. "We can't always take the safest path."

"What's your hurry anyway? Adventure for the sake of it?"

*

The downside of speaking out is that some people feel aggrieved as though I'd criticised them personally. The day after our gathering, I heard my name among the murmurings that seeped across the canteen. People threw glances in my direction but quickly looked away when I tried to meet their eye. I don't think I imagined this. And, yesterday, I sat alone in the meadows. No one chose to join me. Even the home-farmers kept their distance. I'm now half expecting a visit from a medic for a formal assessment of my *contentedness.*

When did we become docile? Is that the right word? Am I being fair? I count back through the previous years' lacklustre leaders: seven in my opinion. Half my life feeling uninspired by our leadership. Is this the right way? Should we choose on merit, vote for someone with a persuasive agenda? Oh, for a leader who makes you feel alive, and heard! A leader worth keeping for a second term, or longer.

Since the gathering, I've been keeping to myself. My provocation might be percolating through our community, and that's an encouraging thought. It may take time for some people to absorb my ideas. In the meantime, I am immersed in the daily chores of the rainforest biome, and I begin the annual survey of bracket fungi. In fact, it's a relief to be busy with detailed work, close observation. I become willingly enfolded in mapping each outcrop of fungus, noting whether the fungus is edible or of medicinal use. I note the host tree, whether that tree is upright and living or fallen and rotting. There is so much *Piptoporus betulinus* on rotting birch that I break off a large hoof of the fungus. I'll give it to the canteen workers as a gift this evening. They will enjoy the delicacy to that particular brew. I'm admiring the hoof, the white cracks on the pale brown upper surface – nature is so unwittingly beautiful – when I hear my name being called. I look up and glimpse Bala through a chaos of hazel trees.

"The earth heals!"

"With our love and care."

"Don't look so surprised. I said I would visit." She pants with the exertion, the humidity. "I plan to do so more frequently." Reaching me, she straightens up and offers a handshake. I take it. She wipes sweat from her forehead. "And I must say that of all the spheres, this is our jewel, our treasure." She takes a swig of water from her carry bottle. "You look suspicious. No need to be."

"I'll show you around then, Bala. You'll want to inspect the glades. See if you agree with the seniors."

"If you tell me that last year's tree thinning is not an issue, I'm happy to accept that. I will report back at the next gathering for the sake of appearances. But yes, do show me what the old-timers are bothered about."

I lead the way. We climb over boulders and fallen branches. I don't rush because I feel I should tease out some joy for Bala on this rare visit. I point out our precious tree lungwort and name the bracket fungi including a spectacular outcrop of hazel gloves fungus. She waves my attention to a small, chequered skipper butterfly. It sits twitching its wings on an oak leaf before darting at speed over a thicket of goat willow. "Well spotted, Bala. And totally good timing for your visit because that particular butterfly needs a sunny habitat within a woodland. Without the glades we'd lose them all."

We reach the largest glade in the biosphere, and I say over my shoulder, "I'm sorry if I pushed too hard at the gathering."

A jay takes flight. "I love a jay!" she says.

I wonder if she heard my apology. "It's our biggest bird here, and it seeds the forest for us. It flies around with acorns, burying them for the future."

She turns to me. "Look, I don't mind you speaking out, but I'd like to finish my term without a revolution." She sighs. "So, what's the problem with this glade?"

"There isn't a problem, as such. We doubled its area by brush cutting and pollarding. It's easy to let the forest encroach. To be frank with you, over recent years no one has taken things in hand. So, when I became head of woodland ecology, I introduced some longer-term plans. If I showed you the drone photos from earlier phases of this sphere, you'd see how we've surrendered too much open ground."

We stand side by side, watching six or seven butterflies – pearl-bordered fritillary – skittering around their roost in the low growth. I'm about to speak but when I glance at Bala, I see she is smiling. Lost in the moment. A childhood memory?

She sighs. "So sweet, aren't they?" And turning to me: "Listen, about the gathering. Your outburst? I have a suggestion for you. I think you need a break from these dank rainforests. Why don't I reassign you to the grasslands for a few months. Call it a sabbatical. Perhaps the open spaces will satisfy this yearning you feel for the outside."

"It's not simply a yearning for the outside. It's also a yearning to test myself, for everyone to test themselves and to interrogate our mission."

"I don't follow."

"We need to take risks. Don't you see? We never shock ourselves. We always lean into safety."

I guide her back to the grasslands. I don't believe she grasped my meaning.

*

My secondment to the grasslands came through two days later. Bala agreed I could finish my fungi survey before I made the move. And with the survey completed, I invited the kitchen team to harvest chicken-of-the-woods, *Laetiporus sulphureus*, from our oak trees. And I urged the clinic to send someone out for the turkey tail fungi, *Trametes versicolor*, for medicinal use. I wanted everyone to see I'd settled back into my work, that they had nothing to fear from me. But when they did arrive to make their collections, no one attempted to speak privately with me. I'd hoped someone would encourage me, agree that we needed a closer connection with the old world. It seemed no one really cared like I did. One thousand acres seemed to be enough for everyone else.

I feel let down, frustrated. I do wonder if we need a mini catastrophe – is there such a thing? – to shake people out of their complacency, their contentedness. If I've failed with rousing words – which seems to be the case – perhaps I should agitate, take action. Dare I? I could never harm my rainforest, but if our home-farm suffered some mishap…

My time in the meadows will allow me to meditate, consider the nature of rebellion, study the saboteurs of olden times. I don't want a revolution. I simply wish to precipitate change.

Production – Pristine White – Pale Green

Tim Major

1924 production diary, cont. from previous journal.

18th Sep^r

The magnificent city. The preparatory work has at times seemed endless! The thick card spires are criss-crossed by bridges that provide ornamentation & structure. The 'panes' of the ink windows are streaked with paint to appear as rays of light upon glass. The city is beautiful but it is hardly ready.

I have adjusted the position of my camera again and again, by minute degrees. I am convinced that there is one position & one position only that will display this utopia as it ought to be.

(Question: How ought it to be, M? Answer: The apotheosis of order. A vision depicting the channelling of productivity into fluid motion, lacking human errors, lacking emphasis on ugly human bodies.)

I will find the correct position and I will not begin filming until I am satisfied.

Later—

Frequently, H insists on watching me as I work. He gets in the way, leaning on his cane and watching with beady eyes. I have told him that one assistant – B, that is – is sufficient and that we require no oversight. I have begged my husband to retreat to the house, to his books and his pipe, as befits his advanced age. But men and their need to oversee!

It is very hot here in my garden studio. Its glass panels ensure adequate light for filming, but sunlight streams in <u>constantly</u>, and there are no shades. The panels are tinged green – a literal greenhouse! – which is ideal for light captured on celluloid. When filmed in monochrome, pale green appears more white than white. It is an unseasonably, unreasonably, warm September, and the greenhouse studio is positively sweltering. I sweat as I work, so I am in shirtsleeves, like B. He and I are the same age, and sometimes I enjoy the fantasy that we are equal. But B's arms and body are strong, and his mind is at peace and free of clutter; more often I celebrate our differences. We celebrate them together.

(If only there were no need for H at all… but I must remember that it is my husband H's money that built this studio. And yet it is surely wrong that he is to take sole credit for our production.)

B & I have determined the ideal angle for the camera – but no celebrations; there is a new problem. When H was absent – napping – we performed a test of the workings of the model city, which is installed at the very centre of the studio in order to capture every available ray of light. B pulled at the hidden threads that control all motion within our city. The boxlike vehicles moved, the signage animated – tremendous! But the citizens are another matter. They snag constantly on their prescribed track. The jerky effect is absurd.

19 Sep^r

This morning I wept as I yanked the threads and the figurines only wobbled. Where is the machinelike order I envisaged?

Dear B tried to comfort me but I would not have it. He is well-meaning and sweet but I know where that leads. I must work instead.

Finally discovered the source of the issue myself. One wax figurine was imperfectly fixed, and the track upon which the citizens are mounted became stuck with each pull of the thread. The figurine is resistant to repair, so I have removed him. The track slides smoothly now, and the gap produced by the absent figure is not noticeable from the angle at which my camera is perched.

B made to toss the removed figurine into the garden, but I wouldn't allow it. I have placed the rebellious fellow within the tallest spire of the city.

Later—
Old H returned to the studio, saw our work, declared it ready. We – or rather, he – filmed our working model city. I was unsettled throughout, despite perfect operation of thread, tracks &c. I halted work and removed the painted 'window' of the spire. Now my displaced wax figurine may see the city below.

Later—
H is furious, yet I stand by my impulse. It is now evident to me that painted windows are <u>absurd</u>. The spire must be rebuilt in glass, or rather a sort of glass I know can be made with melted sugar & syrup. B & I will work on glassmaking tomorrow.

20 Sep^r
Our glass has proved too heavy. We must rebuild and reinforce the entire structure of the city.

21 Sep^r
Work continues. We operate well together, B & I, as an efficient dual machine. We always have, within the studio and without. I know that I have been wrong to indulge in him, but equally I relish the temptation.

23 Sep^r
Completion! The city is more magnificent than ever. Now my citizen in the spire may look down at his fellow citizens in the street, who in turn may look up and see their brother. From behind his sugar glass, he gazes upon the world in awe.

We have captured our city on celluloid. Once again, H insisted on operating the camera.

I would be happy at what we have achieved, but I have been unwell.

24 Sep^r

Dreamt of the displaced figurine last night. No – I dreamt of myself, in his place. I watched clouds of steam below – the hallmark of great industry – and heard the tramp of feet.

When I woke I was panting with fright.

Later—

Even B cannot hide his dismay at my new instructions. H was placated only when I insisted that none of our hired actors need return to our greenhouse studio. They have already played the parts of the inhabitants of the city in close-up, and none will be required to do so again.

I will play the part of the displaced citizen myself.

25 Sep^r

H still refuses to allow me to handle the camera, so I will make do with appearing in my film, a stamp of authorship that cannot be erased. Yet of course I will be unrecognisable. For my appearance as the displaced citizen I wore overalls, a cap with dark wig attached, an inked moustache.

The playacting was a thrill. There is freedom in not being oneself.

My sickness troubles me constantly.

I am not blind. I know what it means.

28 Sep^r

Three days alternating between sickness and dedication to my task. More horror from B & H at my insistence on refilming the footage of the city's inhabitants which will be interspersed among shots of the model.

I have played each part.

I was never happy with the work of our hired actors. They were sombre, and this city is a joy. The freedom of living within a well-built machine! Anonymity is crucial.

I am all of these citizens, and they are all me.

Later—

I am still aghast. When the celluloid was finally bathed and developed, my husband & I watched it on the projector that was installed in his study at great expense, all those many months ago when he first spoke of allowing me to create cinema. (Rather than a gift, I saw it as a territorial act – anything I produced would be analysed, then stamped with his mark before being permitted to go into the world.)

The footage was…

It was not ruined, precisely. But each snippet was marred by the same issue. After witnessing it, I ran to the garden studio to find B sweeping up, and I accused him of bungling the development of the celluloid. He insisted that he knows the chemical process well, which is true. Dear B returned with me to H's study and together we three viewed the other reels which depict the model city, and they are pristine & marvellous. It is only those sequences in which I am the subject that are spoiled.

In each of those sequences, a vertical line of light interrupts the frame. In each case, it bisects me.

I have watched the reels countless times. It is not only the bleached streaks that are disturbing. My face, my expression. What was I thinking about, when the camera lens was trained upon me?

Worst of all is my portrayal of the displaced citizen in the spire. His faraway stare at the unseen street below suggests neither pride nor awe. He is appalled.

And more than that. He is defensive and withdrawn. His hands cradle his belly.

He appears – no, *I* appear – haunted.

30 Sep^r

I have determined that the citizen in the tower is unimportant compared to those figurines affixed to the track. But no closeups are required, certainly not if streaks of light are to lance through them and through my abdomen.

The <u>city</u> is the only story I must tell. The city is a marvel. I only wish that it were real. I am attracted to the idea of industry, of processes working seamlessly – not lacking in human involvement but instead reliant upon it, yet without the petty grievances of usual life. Men & women working in harmony, each in their appropriate place and performing their prescribed function. No inequality. No surprises.

I have jammed the displaced citizen back onto the track countless times. In my tests he is compliant. Yet whenever the camera is operated, he finds some new way to make himself a nuisance. B begs me to dismiss the issue. But he also knows from experience that what I want, I tend to get.

H's patience has worn thin. I am certain he has noticed the way that B looks at me, and understands what it means. He does not speak of it though, and he has drawn no attention to my bouts of sickness or the way my hands frequently drop to rest on my belly. He says only that we must move on, that celluloid is expensive, that reputations are at stake.

He means his own reputation. When this project is complete, it will carry his name. As will anything else I create.

I have slipped my displaced citizen into the front pocket of the overalls that I have taken to wearing daily.

2 Oct

I know that they are worried about me, H & B both. The last several mornings, I have crept to the greenhouse studio before dawn, many hours before B arrives and when H is still snoring in our bed. I have manipulated the camera myself, removing it from its perfect vantage point above the city and balancing it upon crates so that its lens is at street level.

Later—

H was tolerant of my behaviour until this afternoon; now he finally knows that I have been filming the inhabitants of my city, expending yards upon yards of celluloid on recording immobile things of wax. In my excitement to make him understand, I let slip that B has been developing the footage. Despite some reluctance, B accepts that I have a vision of the final film, and a vision of the shape of things to come.

H's response was abrupt and extreme. He swung around to accuse B: —*Waste my time and resources, would you? Lead my wife further into lunacy, would you?* B was steadfast, shaking his head but making no excuses. He is a fine, simple man, which is what inspires my love for him. When H swung his cane, B reached up and took it from him easily. In a rage, H abandoned the cane and threw himself at B.

I should not have become involved, but I forced myself between them, demanding calm. B backed away, H kept coming, and I was trapped in the centre. We all toppled to the floor in a tangle, knocking into the central table and setting my magnificent city rocking. The camera fell from its crates and dropped to the floor with a crash. I crawled over to it to find that its lens was shattered.

Both men reached down to help me to my feet.

But I could not rise. The pain was like nothing I have known. Pain in my head & pain in my womb.

Finally, they sat me upon a stool. They retreated to watch me from a distance. My head hung heavily, and I clutched my aching belly, whispering to it. Until today I have tried to avoid drawing attention to my condition, for fear of H's rage – and for fear of B fleeing due to the certain knowledge that he and I have created this problem together.

When I looked up, B & H were staring at one another in astonishment.

Later—

Upon examination of my city I discovered that many of the sugar-glass windows have shattered, like the lens of the camera. One of the panes must have fallen upon the citizens on their track before breaking, and several of the wax figurines are now badly misshapen.

All of this seems to reflect the fact that I am losing heart in my project. I have no desire to replace either the windows or the people. I was wrong about the glory of pristine white, the pretence of mechanical order. Ruin suits this city.

I have discovered a patch of discoloration at one corner of the model, low down at the cardboard base of the tallest spire. It is mould, pale & green.

4 Oct^r

I have been confined to bed. My thoughts have been occupied with the green mould. In my delirium I have held up my hand to the dimmed gas lamp, my eyes stinging as I regard my thin fingers, which appear tinged green. I know that the same pale algae is within me, and it is spreading.

9 Oct^r

They do not know that I have been returning to the studio. H is old & easily fooled. B is gone, no longer engaged to work on our films.

I have not broached the idea of replacing the camera lens. What need is there for any other person to observe what I have made? I am the creator, and I am here observing my city, every day. If I were to record any footage – if I were to complete production – H would claim ownership.

The mould has taken hold of the city. On each of my visits I have delighted at its progress. The thick card of the spires is rotting. The glass is weeping syrup. The wax figurines are furred with spores.

It is dangerous to enter, but I love this city. It will not allow me to be harmed.

I have brought the camera low once again. Its cracked lens is no matter at all. I will stride along the street towards the spire.

Later—

As I passed them, the eyes of the wax citizens did not meet mine. Instead, they lingered on the front pocket of my overalls, where my displaced citizen rests.

The door of the tallest spire is only an ink outline. Nevertheless, I pushed it open. Inside should be nothing at all, a vertical void, but I climbed the stairs.

I was weary by the time I reached the apartment on the uppermost floor.

This was where my displaced citizen once surveyed the city. Now I stand where he stood and I pat my belly and I look through the sugar glass, which heat and rot has made entirely translucent.

The city below is more green than white. I only wish my camera were capable of capturing the colour. On a cinema screen, the city would still appear white & pristine, if not for the bulbous masses where the mould has bloomed.

Beyond the confines of the city is the darkness of the studio. I see a mass of costumes ready to be worn; bottles of chemicals; set dressings propped up on flimsy stands. Beyond these things are the transparent walls of my studio, tinted green by the rising sun.

And beyond that is the garden. I do not remember the last time I stood in the garden, as opposed to simply hurrying through it in my eagerness to reach the miniature world I have created. And I do not wish to go out there now. Not yet.

I have loved this place.

I have loved.

Later—

I am not high enough above the city. I must find another vantage point, a perfect angle.

Later—

I returned to the stairwell and began the ascent, but the gantry soon ended and I was forced to climb hand over hand along the slippery interior walls.

Finally, I reached the roof.

The view is glorious. The streets below appear as mere diagrammatic representations. The scent of the mould is sweet & comforting. The misshapen heads of the citizens have fallen back and they stare up at me.

For the first time, I have seen birds. Paper birds, caught in flight. Now they have begun to flap their folded-paper wings to resume their course, bisecting the city. I watch them and I am encouraged.

This morning I told myself that I would enter the city and that I would never leave. But that was wrongheaded. It is not me that belongs here.

I dream of other productions – ones that will not bear my husband's name. But first I must see this project to its end.

I am shocked to find that the pocket of my overalls is laced with green. The mould has infiltrated the fabric. I cannot bring myself to touch it, certainly not to push my hand into the pocket.

After I have written this entry, I will put my journal aside. I will take my time. I will gaze down at the city I have built. As I watch, the corruption will spread. The mould will claim the city entirely.

Then it will claim what is in my pocket, and what is in me. They both belong here.

When it is complete, I will walk away from this city, free.

Bittersweet Feast – The Persistence of Swine – To Savour Dawn

Anna Orridge

N34 and his fellow sustenance apprentices were permitted to deviate from sliced cubes on one occasion, and that was the Day of Unanimity.

They still had to adhere to the normal rules of texture and taste, naturally. But they were allowed to engage in a little playfulness of the geometrical variety.

"Do it in much the same spirit as the music factory, aiming for harmony and purity in flavour above all," their tutor D18 had told them.

N34 was excited because the only area he truly excelled in was knife skills. There were not many opportunities to demonstrate this ability, since most days the food was mechanically diced. He started with rectangles arranged across the plate in careful, vertical lines.

"Exquisitely cut, precisely placed," D18 remarked, tapping the side of his very prominent Roman nose, as was his wont when considering something. His odd little grin appeared, a smile with a downward rather than upward curve to the mouth.

"But there is a problem?"

"I suppose it's rather reminiscent of the pipe gradations in an organ..." he shook his head. "My fault, rather than yours. We must, of course, avoid any hint of the figurative."

N34 nodded. He could not show even the slightest indication

of temper. His impatience had been noted on more than one occasion.

D18 laid a hand on his wrist. "It's perfectly salvageable. Just change the arrangement of the lines. You have fourteen minutes before it is due to be cured."

So N34 arranged his strips, not without casting an envious glance at his neighbour – G something. For one whose skills in sustenance were immaculate, G was peculiarly forgettable. At any rate, he had executed a number of perfect trapezes in a variety of sizes.

As he was about to lay his own offering on the conveyer belt to go into the oven, N34 realised his celebratory plate had swapped the appearance of an organ for that of the glass towers of their city. Too late to change it now, though. The dangers of the figurative were everywhere.

*

After the Day of Unanimity, the apprentices were all scheduled to go to a lecture at the auditorium. This one would be about the history of petroleum food.

It commenced with an exhibition of paintings, probably taken from the Old House. The apprentices were allowed to get up and take a close look at them. They were rather grimy, clean light from the glass above slashing the oily surfaces. But N34 could make out bowls of what used to be called fruit, an indecent multiplicity of misshapen forms that could remind one only of swellings and cysts.

They all took their seats after a few minutes.

"Consider," intoned the voice of the lecturer. "So attached were the savages to this form of food, they would *display* it in their homes as a sign of status. Just think of that – a pile of decaying matter, something to be proud of, while insects spurted their digestive juices all over it."

This prompted guffaws from the benches, and not a few snorts of disgust.

"Numbers – know that there was not even ABUNDANCE in this system. The savages often struggled to feed their uncontrolled populations. This led to famine. What will probably truly come as a surprise to you, though, is that they were not unaware of the potential of petroleum. Unlike One State, however, they did not regard it as the clay of sustenance."

A large photograph was carried to the podium. It showed a large square of rough dirt dotted with neatly spaced plants. They were being sprayed with liquid by a large machine of some kind on wheels.

The commentary continued. "They did, in fact, use it as fertilizer – well, not just petroleum, but with petroleum as a base. You heard that right – they squandered one of our most precious resources. Just pouring it out on dirt."

More expressions of disbelief. One number, a young woman with short but very curly hair, laughed hard enough to make her shoulders shake. N34 forced his eyes away from her.

Two days more until he could lower the blinds with anyone.

His teachers told him he had to watch his impetuousness. They were right. He refocussed on the lecture.

"...a century and a half had lapsed before it was realised that petroleum itself could be the sustenance that humanity so badly required after they'd exhausted the soil. It could well be argued that this innovation, before any others, was the one to lay the firmest foundations for OneState. Never let anybody tell you that Sustenance is a lowly calling for a Number. Later today, as you will know from looking at your Tables, you will have an opportunity in lab eighteen to repeat the experiments that led to this breakthrough. Beforehand, please repair to Sustenance Hall B to benefit from the superfluous plates created yesterday."

*

N34 stared down at his plate, a series of intersecting circles which, in his view, had been less than perfectly executed. He plunged his fork in, and realised the texture was wrong too.

There were two permitted textures for sustenance: a jelly-like consistency, one with a little more resistance and bite, probably rather like the flesh the savages used to feast upon. Then there was the hard one. They were not, under any circumstances, to be deviated from or combined.

The apprentice had clearly chosen Hard for his plate, but had allowed it to be cured a little too long, and it was actually gritty against the tongue.

N34 caught a few other Numbers stealing a glance at him – the crunching was loud enough to hear. He swallowed, despite the abrasion, and the discomfort matched what he recognised as his rising irritation. He immediately commenced the steps he'd been taught to calm this anger.

First, the source? Most immediate, of course, was the embarrassment caused by the crunching. But that was not all. He was *enjoying* that sensation. Even now, he could not stop himself pressing one of the crumbs against the palette of his mouth with his tongue to better extract the umami flavour, one of the five permitted.

N34 dropped his fork and got up, leaving too fast to observe the reactions of the other apprentices to his abrupt departure from the Sustenance Hall.

*

At the lab, all had been laid out neatly for N34 along with his fellow apprentices, to make their first attempt at basic petroleum food from scratch. It had, of course, been a long time since human beings had to do any of this by hand. Now it was all performed in the great vats of the Accumulator Tower, everything measured out perfectly and heated with ovens and pressure gauges. But it was agreed that it was best for apprentices to understand the practice as well as the theory.

And so the test tubes and vats were laid out neatly on each bench, the formulae and instructions propped up on lecterns on each desk.

The task required meticulous attention rather than any great cognitive prowess, and N34 found that he could mostly let his mind wander as he completed the stages. He found he had some time to linger on the section he, personally, found most interesting: the construction of flavour.

Sweet, salty, sour, bitter and umami – each plate would be labelled with gradations. But never could the flavours mix. To sully the purity of taste in this way would be akin to combining the notes of the music towers' perfect scales. Sacrilege.

As N34 was lingering on this page, the tutor D18 stopped at his bench to assess his work so far.

"As usual, done with precision. I note you are lingering over flavour... I don't suppose you have ever heard that some tribes of savages swore by the combination of bitter and sweet?"

D18 laughed at his student's moue of distaste. "I know. I know. Habituation from childhood clearly mangled their poor taste buds as much as it mired their intellects. They were so enamoured by that marriage of flavours they would even describe a feeling of happiness tinged with nostalgia as bittersweet."

N34 nodded. "Yes, I remember hearing at one of the lectures that savages drew parallels between flavour and heightened emotional states. It's one of the many reasons why maintaining the purity of flavour is important."

D18 compressed his lips into that downward curving smile. "Well, quite. Just out of interest, there are ways of mingling flavours in our petroleum food, particularly its liquid form. We did once let apprentices experiment with it, early in my career. A practice long since banned, and no doubt rightly so. But since you're quite far ahead this morning, I may as well show you."

D18 went away briefly and came back with the relevant formulae. N34 had cause to look around and noted that most of his classmates had reached the same stage as him, and a few considerably ahead. So why had he been singled out?

There was not much time to ponder this before his tutor came back with the relevant papers and they immediately started working on the formula together.

"Here – this is the one for bittersweet," D18 said, smoothing out the page. "Once you've completed it, you can wave me over and I'll do a quick taste and texture test. Then we'll destroy it promptly, of course."

D18 moved on to another bench.

It was easy enough to follow the formula, and N34 soon had the materials in the crucible, simmering away. He felt an odd urge to look from side to side, furtively, to see if the other apprentices were watching him.

But his rapidly coagulating jelly was much the same vivid yellow as the previous one had been. Besides, why would he feel trepidation? He was simply following his tutor's instructions.

He set the concoction aside to cool, and that was when Y52 entered the lab.

Y52 was a female Number, probably in her early forties. She was senior to D18, and had a far less amiable manner than his tutor. When she entered the lab, backs straightened. Many apprentices leaned closer over their formulae and scribbling accelerated.

N34 was about to place his creation in a container, when Y52 stopped by his bench.

"I'll give that a quick taste test before you pack it up." A crisp command.

N34 felt the blood draining from his cheeks, but he could hardly refuse.

Y52 took a small blade from her pocket and cut a slice of the jelly. As she savoured it, N34 watched her expression change. Her fury, of course, was controlled, and evidenced only by a slight narrowing of the lips.

She did not swallow his concoction. She drew out a tissue from the same pocket the blade had come from, and spat it out. Then she called D18 over.

She jabbed a finger at N34, without looking at him. "This Number just combined flavours."

D18's forehead crinkled in concern. He took a deep breath. "I'm sure that must have been a mistake, he just got the formula wrong and..."

N34 blinked, tried to catch his tutor's eye for reassurance. What did he mean, a mistake? He needed to explain the apparent irregularity immediately.

Y52 snorted. "You know full well nobody can achieve a flavour combination inadvertently... Oh, and here's the proof anyway."

She snatched up a fistful of the papers from N34's lectern. Her eyebrows arched in triumph as she handed them over to D18.

Silence as D18 perused the papers.

N34's heart beat fast. Why on earth would he need to look? He knew exactly what was there.

D18 squeezed his eyes shut. When he opened them, he pinched the skin at the top of his nose between his finger and thumb. "All right. It does appear he has conducted forbidden experiments. Really, it's my fault. I shouldn't leave these sorts of papers just lying around."

Lying around? You handed them to me.

Y52 crossed her arms. "No doubt. But it is the young man here who will pay the price for your carelessness."

N34 wanted to shout, grab his tutor by the collar. Surely, surely this most benign of mentors would not betray him like this? He who had so many times helped him, despite his impetuousness, who had seemed to show him favour even.

But D18 just shook his head, his eyes on his colleague. "Oh come now, surely there's no need to take this further. The lad hasn't had any serious breaches to date."

"Oh, no *serious* breaches, hmm?"

She turned to N34, her expression now bland. "You may leave now. You will be hearing from the disciplinary committee, I suspect by tomorrow morning."

N34 wanted nothing so much as to run his hand across the surface in front of him, send all the glass equipment smashing to the floor. Instead, he picked up his papers, lips dry and eyes stinging with incipient tears.

*

The notification did indeed come the following morning, slanting sunlight pouring across the crisp white paper.

It has been the decision of the committee to suspend the apprenticeship of N34 on the grounds of conduct endangering the purity of his fellow apprentices and the integrity of his chosen profession.

N34 will report tomorrow for duty at the Green Wall, post C. Guard Observer.

Guard observation. In other words, looking out onto the bleak wilderness and checking the forcefield. N34 would never be a sustenance technician.

For the first time in his life, he longed to lower the blinds, not because of the presence of a female Number, but because he wished to hurl things around, tear the paper in his hand to pieces.

He could not stay here, in this room. He needed to get out, breathe, walk.

He chose a route that gave a view of some of the most impressive cluster of towers in the distance.

N34 had been walking for about fifteen minutes when he heard a spatter of footsteps behind him.

He turned. It was D18, his yuni flapping about him as he ran. N34 froze. He was afraid he would not be able to stop himself driving a fist into that beak of a nose, hearing the crack of bone.

But he simply waited instead.

D18 caught up to him. For a half a minute or so, the older man panted, hands on knees. When his breathing slowed, N34 finally got some words out.

"What can you possibly have to say to me that I would want to hear?"

"Nothing. I know you must be furious. I do have something to show you, though. Come."

D18 took one more deep breath and walked towards the Accumulator Tower, waving his hand in invitation.

N34 caught up to him in a few bounds and yanked him back by the shoulder.

"You think I'll just *follow* you?"

D18 laid a warm hand on the one that now scrunched his collar. "Steady. You need to watch that temper of yours."

"Oh yes. I know. That was why you chose me, wasn't it? I know what you're doing. Forcing apprentices to create these perverted concoctions you crave. And, of course, you look for ones like me, with poor records of self-control. So even if I did report you, I would never be believed, you swine!"

D18 smiled, despite the tightening round his collar.

"Swine, hmm? Strange how persistent that word is in the language. You have, of course, never seen a pig in real life. They were reviled, not only for their presumed filth, but because they had a reputation for greed, gluttony. Isn't it strange how we most despise what we know we are most guilty of? Humans have always had that desire to glut ourselves. OneState cannot strip it of us entirely."

N34 was so shocked by this, he loosened his grip on his ex-tutor's collar.

D18 smoothed his yuni down. "You are right. I did single you out. But not for the reason you think. Come."

N34 did follow, past the Accumulator Tower and towards some other slightly shorter, squatter buildings, all topped by domes, where he had often noted the glass was opaque, as if steamed up from inside. He did not consider this strange, though, as it was clearly not a residential area.

The doorman took an unusual amount of care checking D18's ID. He gave N34 a long, appraising look, but let them both through.

D18 led him to a lift and pressed the button for the top floor. "The dome..." N34 murmured.

"Oh, it's a lot more than just a dome."

When the doors of the lift slid open with a gentle chime, N34 let out an expletive and had to steady himself against the walls. D18 laughed. "I know, I know. It's quite something."

The entire room was full of huge wooden containers, each bursting with plants and trees. It was like seeing beyond the Green Wall... only this was right in front of him with no safety barrier. He recognised the darts of colour wafting or streaking amongst the stems as insects. And amongst the branches and leaves – clumps of orange and purple and blue that he recognised as fruit. Along the floor, there were lines of plants, some of them hosting swollen green bodies between the leaves. Above it all loomed that great dome, the sun a clenched fist of white light just at its base, sending streaks across the floor and the heads of the Numbers below. There were around thirty of them, all milling about two tables with serviettes in their hands. They had fallen silent at their entrance, but quickly resumed their animated chatter after D18 raised his hand in reassurance.

A couple of them were circulating with trays. On one of these were piles of gleaming slices, any number of colours.

D18 plucked one that was a very similar bright yellow to the lump of jelly that had got N34 expelled the day before. He put it on a serviette and tried to hand it to the younger man. N34 backed away.

"Please. Eat."

"This could get us all killed," N34 breathed.

"No. Not here. It is sanctioned."

"You cannot seriously expect me to believe the Benefactor would permit this?"

D18 sighed. "Come now. You are not so naïve as all that. Permission is not always a slip freely given or a nod. Sometimes it is an absence of attention. There are a certain number of people who know about this in order for it to all function properly. And, for our silence, we are granted certain... privileges. In short, we are allowed to experience taste as the savages would have done."

"But it would take an awful lot of failure of attention to get this many plants and vegetables here from the outside." N34 was conscious his voice was rising far above that of the gentle murmur of conversation. Yet he attracted only a few sharp glances from those around him. Failure of attention was clearly a common skill amongst these honoured few.

D18 laid a hand on his arm. "No, no. You misunderstand. These were all here from the very beginning of OneState. We collect seeds and bulbs to propagate them."

"But why?"

D18 took a deep breath. "Has it not ever occurred to you that there is something faintly ridiculous about the story of food created from petroleum? Petroleum, the product of long dead and crushed animal and plant matter, its energy only released by burning? My dear N, it was not turned into food. What we call sustenance is very much the same as what was grown and consumed by human beings in the times of savagery. It is convenient that our structures are built of glass, because many fruits and vegetables flourish in the heat that accumulates within. Although many of the topsoils around the world had been greatly diminished, we were fortunate to find a few in the Northern hemisphere that remained reasonably rich. We transported them, and we keep them replenished with compost. This is one of four great greenhouses in the city. Once the vegetables and fruit are grown, they are boiled, combined with the correct ratio of proteins and turned to the flavourless pulp you have been used to. There is actually some petroleum used in it – paraffin, but purely to aid the speed of digestion."

"Why on earth would you tell me all this?"

D18 put a hand on his arm. "Look. I said you were chosen. And yes, you were chosen for your impetuousness, your lust for life. You are perfect for this work."

D18 held out, again, the slices. They gleamed wetly in the light, like the backs of fish glimpsed in a river. N34 could see the fibres, the natural imperfections of the cut that somehow made it even more enticing. He took the serviette.

D18 smiled and nodded. "Please. Taste. What is in your hands was once called mango. Even if you decide you are not going to work with us, you deserve this experience. I owe it to you."

N34 raised the slice to his lips and was stunned by the intoxicating scent. If the first rays of dawn could have a scent, this was it.

His hands trembled. What would happen to one who dared to savour dawn?

In Praise Of TwoState – Epiphanies – The Morning After

Douglas Thompson

A great battle hymn is required, our glorious leader has decreed, an epic ode in praise of TwoState. I devoutly hope that I am up to the task. I have read all the dystopias envisaged by past generations, the novels by those Orwells and Huxleys and Bradburys, and I laugh heartily at how wrong they all got it. Always they envisaged a regimented future in which we all wear uniforms and act like machines and are denied choice and free will. Then along comes a woman (always a woman and always a sexually attractive one) – to bring about the fall of the authoritarian utopia, by leading astray our hitherto conventional male protagonist. But let me assure you, let me show you how the future is nothing like that, by leading you through one day of our fabulous lives, my life here in TwoState.

Every morning I wake at the same time. I do not need an alarm clock, no state-controlled bell or flashing red light. I rise ridiculously early at 5.15 a.m. entirely of my own volition through years of self-imposed discipline and experience, knowing as I do that my employer may wish us both to sally forth from our office at 7.30 a.m. I need to leave myself enough time, plus a safety margin, to arrive at the office in readiness at 7.00 a.m. once public transport has conveyed me there. You see, there are two of everything in TwoState, hence its name. Two types of people, let's start with that. Those with excess money and time, and those with very little of either. My employer is of the former class and I am of the latter.

Hence why he can live in the city centre, only a short walk from our office, while I must live a long way out in a downbeat suburb and laboriously travel back and forth each morning and night on buses and trains. And as is the way in TwoState, *our way*, these two factions, as every other pairing, are pitted against each other in a perpetual tension and ever-bubbling struggle beneath the surface. Thus those who drive the buses and trains frequently have strikes and work-to-rules and various forms of protest in order to try to extract pay rises and concessions from their employer and the governing class above them. Thus I have to get up even earlier each morning, to mitigate the risk of these strikes delaying my journey in, and leaving me the fallback option of walking in even in the pouring rain if need be, to fulfil my ongoing undertaking of undying unreliability to my employer. But do please remember, dear reader and ignorant citizen of the unenlightened societies of the past, that I do all of the foregoing, and the following, entirely of my own free will, without any fear of being beaten across the back with high-tech electrodes by the fascist boot-boys of utopia.

No, TwoState is much kinder, much more benign, and much more cunning than that. We all know our place. We never riot or loot, we never storm the organs of government and string the overlords from lampposts. That would be so impolite and unseemly. My wife gets to sleep on for a while because her employer allows her to work from home for half of the week. What could be kinder and more benign of them than that? And yet, this concession fills her with so much guilt and over-compensation that she works through her lunchbreaks and long into the evening each night, lest her colleagues or employer should think that she is not getting enough work done during the day and sitting around skiving. You see? How brilliantly TwoState polices itself? The secret police, our KGB, *our Stasi*, are ourselves. The censorship has all gone underground, operating internally in the brain, thus leaving no room for anything else, no secret rebel force of rogue neurons to hide there. Raisa and I have no children, probably for a similar reason, because fifteen years ago when it might still have been biologically possible, she was too scared of how her employers might frown on her and resent her for taking parental leave. And yet, note this was her own choice, not theirs.

Today I walk down our rather rundown and neglected street towards the train station, and there I stand on the platform and notice that the stranger who comes and stands next to me is dressed similarly to myself, in dark grey cargo trousers and grey hooded anorak, and I wonder how this can come about when there are so many clothes shops and online outlets to choose from. Next three different guys, each from the slightly posher side of town, walk down one by one onto the platform, and each of them, quite incredibly, is wearing the same red ski jacket, chosen to make them appear of the managerial class and given to taking alpine ski holidays. This reminds me in turn of the red corduroys that my employer wears, that his fellow posh friends all wear (in various shades from pink through to burgundy and terracotta, the trousers of class war) in their wealthy residential historic district in the centre of town. Then a young woman comes onto the platform, then another two, then three. It is summer. I am able to see that every one of them has a tattoo on her shoulder and at least one on each ankle. This was unheard of twenty years ago but now is *de rigueur*. No law has enforced these fashion codes to be adopted. And yet the serfs, the slaves, citizenry of the future are all in uniform! Oh glorious TwoState! Finally some young men come onto the platform, each wearing shorts and training shoes without socks. I know some of them by sight from regular travel at this time, and know that they wear these same shorts even in the depths of winter, even when pouring with rain or snow. Such is their devotion to the mysterious, invisible tyrant who dictates their sartorial choices.

When I was younger a human being manned this station and made announcements regarding how late the train you were waiting for might be running. But TwoState shuns such antiquated obsolescence. Now on this platform people queue up, not to buy tickets from a human being but from a machine by the simple expediency of flashing their mobile phone in front of it. I have seen them all doing this, even on days and moments when there is an actual person waiting to serve them behind the desk inside the waiting room. Such is their terror of having to face another human being rather than interact with a machine. The details of how late the train we're waiting for is running are conveyed by digital messages on a board overhead, which gradually get more ominous, until now quite suddenly and without warning, the *22 minutes late* message changes to *next train in 41 minutes*. Has the train we're awaiting been cancelled? No explanation will ever be given and there will be no one to ask questions of. Everyone on the platform looks stunned, like the proverbial heads without chickens. Having bought digital tickets that they can't now get refunded, they have no choice but to wait and wait to get their money's worth of agonising waiting. I am however prepared for this, having bought no ticket, and simply set off on foot to walk down into the city, still within my margin of mishap for arriving on time at the office.

On the way down I walk through worrying districts, high-rise concrete blocks, flyovers and underpasses, windswept hard shoulders next to the howling fumes of motorways. No-man's land. Dead zones and grass verges clogged with years of litter, lifeless margins where hypodermic needles gather in droves like windblown pine cones, the detritus of despair. Used nappies are caught like fluttering shuttlecocks on the reverse side of galvanised steel fencing enclosing back courts that nobody ever uses other than for nefarious deeds after dark. I am confused as to whether this fencing is to keep the inhabitants of these houses in or to keep intruders out. Walls carefully re-rendered in graffiti-proof paint nonetheless receive fresh graffiti weekly, surely a glorious confirmation of the endless inventiveness of youth and the technological prowess of paint companies in TwoState. On the main streets, betting shops proliferate, giving the poor a dizzying choice of ways in which to throw away what little money they have left each week. Choice is everywhere. A good choice of chemists in which to have your methadone administered under supervision in a small green cup, or to go away and take heroin instead until your venous system is wrecked and your legs need to be amputated. You can still smoke until your lungs give out and drink alcohol until your liver packs in, via a thousand different brands backed by multi-million dollar industries and by government of course via taxation. Stern health warnings are given on labels, but the consumer, that ever-savvy citizen of TwoState must always be left to make his own choices. We trust him so much, we believe him to be wise. His rights and freedoms must always be respected. Self-destruction, even suicide is a choice after all, and possibly a surprisingly attractive one when you have no job, no self-respect, and not enough money to live on. Food banks proliferate, a healthy growth industry in TwoState. In these districts everyone adopts the same uniform by unspoken consensus so that the police can arrest them more easily: tracksuits for adults, hoodies for juveniles.

Nearing the city centre I drop into a supermarket to buy my lunch in advance and am amazed as ever by the dizzying choice of everything. A visitor from another planet would surely be terrified by this spectacle, regardless of whether they had mastered our language. Which of a dozen toothpastes to choose? Which of fifty breakfast cereals? Which of a hundred biscuits? And here are blackberries, picked by starving peasants in Bolivia the packaging proudly tells me, and shipped six thousand miles across the Atlantic Ocean, while the self-same fruit sits on the hedgerows around every suburb and rots on the vine here until it is eaten by birds or rodents. Six thousand miles of airline fuel versus a short stroll that might save you your gym membership? No contest apparently in TwoState. The consumer must have perfect fruit and choice in abundance.

Arriving at work at last, just in time, I jump into the passenger seat of my employer's Ferrari and am whisked away through the still early morning streets towards our latest project. The engine roars as he needlessly overtakes everything else that dares to move. I am reminded of the increasing rarity of this guttural sound, anachronistic, like the lonely roar of a mastodon assailed by cavemen, the kind I remember from my textbooks at primary school. Electric cars quietly pass us, Amazon drones purr overhead as they ceaselessly deliver gifts to those bored by excess money and time. Deliveroo rickshaws rattle by, driven by exhausted illegal immigrants without passports or employment rights, taking a coffee and two doughnuts to a flat three miles away whose occupant chose not to benefit from the one minute stroll to the coffee and doughnut shop under their window. But for all the participants in this peculiar transaction, it was their choice and they were all magnificently free to make it, including the choice to cross the English Channel in a leaky dinghy. We are such a great place to live. Long live TwoState.

While talking idly about the late trains, my employer asks me why I don't drive a car and I find, perversely, that I am too ashamed to tell him I can't afford one because he doesn't pay me enough. This is similar to when he asks me why I don't have children, and I am too ashamed to admit that my wife was too timid to entertain the notion and its financial impact. No such fear for him, who has put three children through education at an expensive private school, partially paid for, one must logically extrapolate, from the fruits of my labours.

We arrive at the house we are working on. The refurbishment of an A-listed historic building into a luxury pad for the super-rich. I get my tools out and begin sawing wood and firing studs and battens up with hammer and nail gun, forming new walls for luxury ensuite bathrooms. I am the muscle and the hard-graft. I just let my boss do all the talking to the clients. The bored and idle wife of some wildly rich businessman who spends half his time in the Middle East, who is given a budget to pointlessly rip out her kitchen and bathrooms every four years to put in new ones, just to keep up with changing fashion trends. Today the boss is expecting a difficult conversation since the rich wife has been moaning recently that the kitchen we finished last month doesn't look quite "bang on trend". But all is well. She relates that a friend of hers walked in on Sunday and told her it was the best thing she's ever seen since last Tuesday. Thereby saving her perhaps twenty grand in our fees, on a whim. It just took someone else to form her own arbitrary opinion for her.

At tea break there is a rare political discussion between the plumber and electrician, which I do my best to stay out of.

TwoState is split into regions for administrative purposes, the two largest of which are North and South. We are in the North, and all love the North, but the plumber supports a football team which passionately wants the South to dominate the North and make all its decisions for it. The electrician supports a football team opposed to all that, who wants the South's domination over the other regions to dissolve so that they can govern themselves. After listening for a while I conclude that it's not a political discussion after all, just one about football teams, since they are both simply supporting the sides that their fathers did as some kind of token of nostalgic allegiance. Then they start talking about religion, different sects of the same fairy tale, but since neither of them are religious I reach the conclusion that they're still talking about football. TwoState is governed by divide-to-conquer. Everyone is required to take a side, even if they haven't a clue what the other side is talking about.

Division is everywhere. Choices, choices. But who am I to talk? In my lunchbreak I go to visit my mistress, Paula. Sometimes we just talk and eat sandwiches and drink orange juice together, and on other occasions we take all our clothes off and bounce away happily on top of each other in her bed. When she's out of breath I get to see that very cute little gap between her front teeth, but the nicest thing is just talking together afterwards and stroking her long blonde hair as it falls across my chest and we take turns to gaze at the ceiling and talk in philosophical platitudes. Today she just wants to talk I see, and unfortunately the talk quickly takes an unexpectedly serious and sobering turn. She says she wants to stop seeing me. That she doesn't want me to leave my wife after all. That she wants to try and get back together with her estranged husband whom she hasn't seen in two years. I expect myself to be able to handle this. I expect myself to have been expecting this. Except. It hurts. Hurts more than I expect. It was she who sought me out, *seduced me*, if you want to use the old-fashioned parlance from the history books. Now what was I saying about all those dystopian novels? How it's always a woman who trips the hero up, the forthright striding male lead, makes him fall flat on his face and discover the previously obscured and thoroughly disquieting truth about himself and his life and everyone else's life within the shaky cardboard construct of society? Oh glorious TwoState in which we are so free to make our own mistakes and discover these wonderful insights!

As I reach for my jacket and prepare to go, a terrible sadness and bitterness is beginning to weigh heavily on me. I thought this affair was just a thing to joke and laugh about, to snigger about with vague hints and never enough detail, down the pub with my mates. But I didn't take account of the hormones, the dopamine and endorphin. All hardwired to the heart, the old goddamned human heart. I have fallen in love with her, but realised only too late, at the end, just as we're ending. And now I see I was only a plaything for her, her bit of rough. Then I remember that she said she went to private school, like all the boss's kids, and that I don't count for her, am not real or to be taken seriously. That I am like a tradesman. She'd see me out the tradesman's entrance if she had one. She's *one of them* underneath it all in other words, despite her gradually concealing her accent over the years. She's a poshy, on the other side from me. Because this is TwoState, in which you can only be one or the other, and there is always two of everything and nothing in between, and choice isn't just a choice, it's a holy maxim, an obligation. No falling between the cracks, the tracks, no fruitless search for mythical middle ground. Lover boy, toy boy, your day in the sun, your roll in the grass is over. Oh glorious TwoState, how I welcome your divine division and internalise it. I am riven.

All the long sickening ride home on the bus that evening I reflect on the split that has been inside me for a long time, and will stay there for many years to come before it heals, if it ever heals at all. Because I have led a double life while pursuing the affair with Paula, going home everyday and living a lie, acting as if everything is fine with Raisa, as if butter wouldn't melt, no matter where you put it. But it's not that simple. If Raisa never knew and never does then it's not her I've hurt, it's myself. A mortal wound, a gaping hole opening up in my chest, spilling invisible emotionalism all over the bus floor. Because I can't go back. I can't forget. I can't unmake all of the things I've done and felt over the last six months.

It was only sex, maybe, except that it's never only sex. Body and mind inextricably intertwined by whatever devil made us all. The dreams unfinished, the fabled hope of escape towards some other life, one less drab, one always made bright by distant shafts of sunlight falling on fragments of glittering seas. I want to scream out loud where I sit alone at the back of the bus. Because who can I ever tell? Not my macho friends down the pub who'd rate it less than tummy trouble and prescribe Irn-Bru. But these are the glorious choices available to us in TwoState. How wonderful to have made my life into a porn movie, a comedy, a tragedy then a horror movie. I want to commit suicide. The rest of my life will be one long tormenting let down. I may never feel true passion again. And then it comes to me at last out of nowhere: that all the Orwells and Huxleys and Bradburys of history weren't using women as a metaphor to help them parody future dystopias at all. They were using future dystopias as a metaphor for extramarital affairs. Now surely only amid the wonderful freedoms of TwoState could a man stumble upon an insight as profound as that one. But who to tell?

Arriving home late due to the train strike and bus detour, I am busy preparing my face to meet the face I am about to meet. Preparing to murder and create, if indeed each man kills the thing he loves, a brave man with a sword, a coward with his tongue unable to speak a word of truth. Yet before I unlock the front door, Raisa swings it open for me and smiling broadly tells me to keep my shoes on because we need to go right back out there now and pop down the road to vote. *Vote? Oh yes*, I say, pleased to have a topic other than my own internal apocalypse to conjure with. *I forgot all about that. Is that today, the general election and all that?* And so we go, not quite hand in hand because we gave that up years ago, along with spontaneous or remotely regular intercourse, but I still realise that I love her. Realise that I am grotesquely ashamed of the wretch I have been and am, and how little I have ever deserved this supremely good and wise creature at my side filling my life with light each day, ignorant of my corruption, innocent in sublime contrast to my own inner ignominy.

We turn the corner and reach the church hall with its temporary booths set up inside, and here comes the sublime moment of triumphant affirmation of the glory of TwoState. Our names are ticked off the register and we go into separate booths as if doing something shameful or dirty and there is a long list of choices we can make, candidates we can put forward to run our future for us on our behalf for the next five years. It could all be quite bewildering, were it not for the fact that almost everyone knows that every single name on the list, except two, would be completely pointless to vote for because they could never win. Still, long live TwoState.

After dinner, Raisa is puzzled by my newfound interest in politics and why I've chosen to stay up the entire night. Yes, the ENTIRE night, watching the election results coming in with bottle after bottle of beer in my hand. Soon I'm shaking and crying and crying, and hoping the sound of the television is drowning the sound of my snivelling. Not that I care about politics, or care who's going to win. But because I'm thinking about Paula and how I'll never see her again, and listening to music in my earplugs, songs she used to play me, sad love songs that seem to be about us, sentimental torture, you know the sketch, as I dredge and plough up my own insides with a combine harvester of regret and self-loathing.

And then as the first light is creeping under the curtains and the birds are starting up their symphony outside I start noticing the results on the telly and I see that the other guys are going to win for a change, for the first time in about twenty years, first time maybe even since before Raisa and I were married. And I see their leader smiling and brushing the dust off his shiny new suit and preparing to go up to the podium to make his first speech to all his millions of followers and the whole country that is about to be led by him. Then it dawns on me. The second epiphany in as many days! He's talking now and smiling at the camera and he's already subtly backing down and reneging on every single meaningful promise he made during his election campaign. I see that his entire journey from member of parliament, to party leader to first minister and president has just been a transformation, like a spider shedding its skin, in which he and his colleagues have slowly become exactly the same as the people they are about to replace. You see? This is the final triumph of TwoState; its greatest sleight of hand, it's most ingenious achievement. In the end all the choices are illusions. There is no real choice. Only the deeply important deception that every citizen *feels* they have made a choice.

Indeed the people are free and their media are free. But the media are so adept at misinformation, ably abetted by the state, that ultimately the citizens will always make the choices the state really wants them to make. When someone comes along genuinely wanting to change things, to end the war between rich and poor, between men and women, then the media will have them utterly discredited soon enough. Dressed in a dunce cap and shoved off to the dunce corner for *not getting it*. And I get it now well enough. That I am just a hairy monkey in a suit, whose entire hard-won intellect can be swayed by the smile and wink of one pretty girl nodding towards her bed. That we are all monkeys, who let the worst of us lead us every time, because the best of us are too busy being distracted and too modest to want power. And that power always drives whoever has it mad, be they good or bad they'll be bad and mad by the end of it because that's what the focus of adoring human attention does to you: makes you drunk and delusional and dreaming that you're God. Except that none of us are or ever can be. God is just an old myth in a forgotten book, who was said to get angry at our hubris and strike down our towers of Babel every time we tried to raise them too high. And when will we ever build a tower that is allowed to stand? When we build one on sound foundations, perhaps. When we build one that is just.

Buoy – Perfect Citizen – Mother

Nadya Mercik

YOUR COUNTRY TAKES CARE OF YOU!

PERPETUUM HAPPINESS OF ITS PEOPLE IS THE
PURPOSE OF THE GOVERNMENT

PURE MINDS – PERFECT CITIZENS – GREAT
NATION

BORDERS ARE A SANITARY MUST!

GREAT RUSOVIA STANDS ON ITS OWN FEET

WE ARE THE SECOND NOAH'S ARK. THE FINEST IN
THE BEST NEW WORLD.

*

Olga stood on the twenty centimetre-wide white line that separated
the righthand side current of people from the lefthand side, one
foot in front of the other, like a gymnast on a balance beam, to
avoid being swept away. Several people had already noticed her
strange behaviour and were obviously wondering why she wasn't
on the crossing island, which was only twenty paces away. But she
couldn't move.

She looked at the processions of people and saw the flaws — somebody a centimetre ahead of his fellow walkers, another out of step with the rhythm of the whole, a set of too-loud, jarringly noisy heels. The perfect organisation of humanity was breaking apart. No, Olga realised, it was she who was broken. The out-of-period bleeding had stopped, but there was still a tugging pain in her abdomen, crawling through her like an eel in the mud.

Her hands instinctively went to her tummy and she felt for any strange hardness but there was nothing — just the sensation of an empty sack. As though, only recently, her tummy had been full. Yet, if anything was seriously wrong, surely she'd get a notification on her subdermal? Besides, she'd just been to the Sanatorium for her bonus Rejuvenation Sleep after the Rotational FemLeave. So she had to be well. The pain simply had to be a figment of her imagination. But how come there were all those folds of skin and unevenness under the fabric and why did her uniform stretch so tightly over her breasts? You were supposed to lose weight in the Sanatorium, not gain it.

A pedestrian on the right collided with her elbow, ruining her balance — the round buoy of her body was almost untethered and pulled into the current. Olga curled her toes inside her shoes, like it could help her have a stronger connection with the white line. But it wouldn't last forever — she had to decide where to go. Yet neither home, nor work, not even the small café with the view of the Fontanka River, where she liked to read a book, were "her" places anymore. The whole city felt alien, exuding animosity, hostile.

The subdermal heated and displayed a message. In a quarter of an hour her shift began; if she didn't hurry up, she'd be late. The school logo disappeared, substituted by the rolling menu. Borscht, mashed potatoes and cutlets, and for the afternoon tea — cottage cheese bake and kompot drink. Her assistant Mila must already be there, pulling out the pots and pans, setting the programmes on the cooker and ovens. Olga suddenly longed to file a migraine, which her subdermal wouldn't be able to recognise, and to dive into the wrong current, then another wrong one, until she ended up somewhere on the outskirts of the city, maybe even further away.

But she couldn't. Not because the subdermal would trace her location. But because of this feeling of a super-thin, almost ethereal fibre running from the top of her head, down her spine, into her belly and then… outwards – an artery pulsing with blood, a power cord, a cable that was transmitting into the void.

Olga felt dizzy and nauseous, her head hurt – as if a giant child was shaking it like a rattle, knocking something inside her brain unconscious. She felt a warm wetness gathering between her legs and looked down to see that the fabric of her trousers had gone dark. She should get into one of the currents. If she just stood on this line, she might bleed to death.

She took a step, toppled into a mass of people – a once comforting and structuring mass. She yearned for the connection and yet the contact, when it came, felt hard and jostling even when a man caught her gently, signalling the need for medical assistance; even when they enveloped her in a tight ring murmuring compassion. She was trying to ask them for fresh air and space – so that the signal her detached cable was sending could go through. Her subdermal singed with basic medication, yet the world was slipping away still, the only tangible thing was the incorporeal cord with no attachment.

*

The Kronversky Prospect was busy with the night shift ending; people hurried alongside Slava in neat parallel rows to comply with their schedules – some went home, others to begin their morning duties. Slava allowed his legs and the well-calibrated Citizens' Circadians to carry him onwards as he looked up at the sky. He almost regretted he couldn't have all his shifts at night during the white night period. By now, the sun was already pretty high, despite the early hour. It gave everything a thick honey quality, turning the city into a gleaming hive. There wasn't a trace of that soothing whiteness the long twilight possessed. The whiteness gave Slava clarity and contentment – even the worst deadlines felt manageable when the skies were like baked milk. Perhaps, his vigour during this period came from the fact that he was born on a white night. Unproved, yet who but him should know about the mysteries of the birth process.

His shoe hit something, and a throbbing pain spread through his toe. Slava came to a halt, finally looking in front of him. For some reason the people had stopped in their tracks. A few were now moving backwards and to the side, as if a pipe had burst in the middle of a walkway. Tall as he was, he couldn't see to the epicentre of the incident. Citizens behind him were trying to adjust to the blockage and the reversal of the current, which only caused more jostling, elbowing and trampling. Slava felt his satchel being pulled as the throng became more compressed and unstructured. Thighs and shoulders brushed against his sides – an unsanctioned, chafing contact. Slava wanted to step away, to escape, but there was no space, no corridor. He could only wait till the conundrum was solved and the well-oiled cogs of the morning march were resumed. What could have happened? It wasn't the right season for frost to rupture a pipe. Besides, he would see the fountain of water. He witnessed it once when he was five and their Hatchery group went to visit the State Museum. But since then the pipe materials had been improved manifold. A sabotage? But those belonged to newspaper archives and the times before the Deflecting Borders were completed; when enemies of the State carried out meaningless acts of rebellion.

"Medical assistance required," sounded a voice from up front – the epicentre of the commotion.

Slava frowned. How could someone have taken ill so suddenly with the Subdermal Prophylactic running? Could the subdermal be malfunctioning? His training, however, took over; he might have spent the last decade doing research, but he'd taken the Hippocratic Oath.

"Let me through!" Slava gripped the strap of his satchel and began to shoulder his way through the crowd. "I am a doctor."

With difficulty, people in front of him were parting. Their expressions, however, betrayed relief. Now they had a specialist amongst them, the problem would be solved in no time.

Slava reached a small circle – inside lay a crumpled body of a plump, young woman. Her features were plain, no make-up, dull, brown hair gathered at the back with pins; her uniform bore a school chevron but she wasn't a teacher. His eyes scanned further down, but even before he saw the small pool of blood gathering below her pelvis, he knew what this was all about. The shape of her full breasts, the protuberance of her belly, could only mean one thing. Slava kneeled and pressed his thumb to the special points around the subdermal, activating the FemRegime. Created for a slightly different purpose, it wasn't a solution, but it would work better than the standard meds for bleeding. As Slava pulled out his phone and dialled his hospital for the special ambulance, he wondered why the woman's subdermal hadn't sent her a warning beforehand. Was it another symptom of failing Erasure?

"I can hear it…" the woman mumbled deliriously. She shifted, more blood pooling between her legs. "…the beat. So strong. No, don't cut it, let it be!" Her arms began to flail. "Why won't you let us be whole?"

Slava felt his own heart freeze for a moment. He'd witnessed such ravings in the past, but he'd driven them out of his mind – nowadays they were nothing more to him than dry medical descriptions. Words on paper. Not anymore.

There seemed to be a strange echo to the woman's pleading – as if her words were reaching some sort of a wall and reverberating off it. As if there were a second party to her monologue, demanding a conversation. Like a ghost of a reply that shouldn't be coming through. A shiver ran down Slava's spine. The protocol of the standard procedure was muddled in his mind. His eyes were glued to the woman's face, but instead of reading her physical symptoms, he saw the worries and smiles behind the lines and dimples; the comfort of round cheeks; the Morse code of the fluttering eyelashes; and just on the edge of her chin – a tiny birthmark. They screamed volumes at him, blurring his idea of a patient, the image of a person as biological unit. A body to study.

A shocked young female voice came from behind him, bringing Slava back to reality. "What is she talking about?"

"She must be hallucinating because of the blood loss," said an older woman trying to calm the younger one, though she didn't sound so sure herself.

They don't know – they'll never know what this is about, thought Slava.

"She'll be all right," he said loudly, finally unclenching his teeth. "The ambulance is on its way."

Seconds later the siren sounded from the Kamennoostrovsky Prospect side. It would be bare minutes now. People began to rearrange themselves, some having to cross onto the wrong side of the walkway. Slava could see how the emergency car with the orange strip instead of the red stopped at the curb and male paramedics with the special Cuckoo emblem on their uniforms climbed out of it. They exchanged knowing nods as the body was loaded onto the gurney.

"You coming with us?" asked the senior.

"Wouldn't say no to a lift." Slava attempted a chuckle, but his throat still felt constricted.

They packed into the ambulance. Slava had to sit at the back with the woman and the other paramedic. He looked through the window trying to focus on the stout grey buildings flashing by. Yet he could still see the woman's face reflected in the glass… calling.

*

The clamps were in place on the white-yellow tube of the umbilical cord. Dr Blinov cast one quick glance at the drugged mother before cutting through it. A meagre quantity of blood stained the latex of his gloves, like unruly jam coming out of a doughnut.

The first nurse – a man, of course, for all nurses were male – handed him the Pulse Disconnector. Dr Blinov always treated the mother first, so that she didn't get in the way of him and the baby. He placed the thin spatula-like ending of the Disconnector into the cut umbilical cord and pushed it deeper as the first nurse removed the clamp on the mother's side. His thumb rolled the trackball regulating the length and strength of the pulses which would go through the placenta and into the mother's body before the former was discarded. He alternated between the programs – it was important to remove the connection between the mother and child on all levels before the doctors touched their minds. It always amused him how even the ejected placenta could leave an imprint on the personality. Dr Blinov cleansed everything thoroughly before turning his attention to the baby.

"Roll the mother off to the Smoother," he ordered without looking at the second nurse, "we were the first Caesarean on the shift – there should be no queue for Scar Removal. And remember Dr Nikolaev is on his annual leave, so there were changes in the Memory Anaplasty rota."

Dr Blinov didn't see the second nurse nod – his whole attention was on the wrinkly baby while he removed the clamp and pulled the umbilical remnants onto the Disconnector. The girl scrunched her face as he began the pulses, though she couldn't be feeling a thing. It was all painless and beneficial. Without the emotional imprints, she would be able to form the correct attachments and attitudes, be a proper individual – a perfect citizen! No dependencies, no ancestral trauma, no attachment disorders, no personal influences – a clean separation, freedom.

He pulled the device out and picked from the tray a single optical fibre ending in a tiny bulb-shaped chip. He pushed the Citizen Filament down the cord as far as he could, then began to squeeze the umbilical to drive it even further. As he tied a plastic cord around the cut end of the umbilical he almost envied her – in his childhood there was no technology to bind him stronger to the community, to make him one with his country. Dr Blinov drew the five-point star on the slimy head of the newborn, blessing her insertion into the Great Rusovia State – that most glorious of nations, alive with the beating hearts of millions! He might not have received the Filament when he was born, but he had plenty of devotion to cover that drawback. *He* was the one delivering the perfect citizens to the State.

Idly, he wondered if the random family name generator might

bestow upon the girl his patronymic. But then he dismissed the pleasant thought. The chances were slim.

*

Four babies later, Dr Blinov was in his office for a well-deserved lunch break. He placed down the cup of coffee, the invigorating bitterness scalding his throat, and reached for his sandwich with a thick slice of cured salmon when someone knocked on the door.

"Come in!" He sighed and pushed the plate away.

The tall, lanky figure of Dr Dubrovsky crossed the room and took a seat without an invitation. Dr Blinov frowned.

"To what do I owe the pleasure, Vyacheslav?" He interlaced his fingers and rested his joint fist on the desk.

"Have you read the daily report, Sergey?" asked Slava. "There is a new case of—"

"I had five scheduled Caesareans. Unlike you, I deal with the real procedure, and we've got a Quarterly Plan to fulfil."

Slava's lips curled derisively, parted for a retort but at the last moment he paused. He'd been a student and protégé of Blinov's once, but over time Sergey had come to detest the man. After the obligatory two years of practice, Slava had left his team and taken up a researcher post in the obscure field of soul; the as-yet-undetected twin of consciousness which could, hypothetically, impact the Umbilical Erasure.

"A woman – Olga Rachmaninova – collapsed today in the middle of the street with a postpartum bleeding just days after your Smoothing. She was raving about the connection to her child. All this happened in front of my eyes." Slava's jaws went stiff. "It's the seventh case this quarter in Petrograd. Your Memory Anaplasty has become less efficient. You can't ignore this!"

Blinov's knuckles cracked as he pressed his hands too tightly together. "My department delivers the best service on every stage. These women are monitored and treated since the moment they are brought here from the Prenatal Facility. If you are looking for faults, maybe you should check how Carers are dealing with their subjects throughout the nine months of their Rotational FemLeave. Maybe, it's their Trance Capsules that interfere. Or something is not right with the Rejuvenation Sleep afterwards so that the Memory Anaplasty is compromised. I vouch for every Birth, Smoothing and Anaplasty performed here."

Slava rose to his feet and leaned forward. "Whoever's fault it is, this needs to be addressed. Do you believe it won't be brought to the Patriarch's attention if women outside the Zero-Interference Birth Group start remembering? And what if the Patriarch decides that all those children born from these women are faulty?" Slava's Adam apple bobbed vigorously, and Dr Blinov felt his own airways constricting.

"What do you want me to do?!" Sergey cried.

Slava wore a rather sour mien when he answered. "Let me back into the surgery to dig deeper. Maybe I've missed something in the EEG, scans and other data. Maybe I… need to get my hands bloody again."

Dr Blinov wasn't thrilled with the offer, but on reflection he realised that this would give him a chance to turn Dubrovsky into a scapegoat if things became worse.

"Fine, I'll put you on the rota, starting tomorrow." Sergey pulled back the plate with his sandwich, but Vyacheslav wasn't leaving. "What else?"

"Ol— I mean, Rachmaninova. Let me run some tests on her before you ameliorate her memory for the second time. I need… We need clues."

"Very well. That's if they haven't started on her already." Sergey waved off his permission, and Slava finally walked out of his office.

The sandwich managed to dry while they were talking, and the rapidly cooling coffee left an unsavoury aftertaste. As Dr Blinov chewed on the bread and salmon after his visitor left, he pulled up Rachmaninova's file on the computer. Everything looked perfect – she had the best neuroplastic surgeon and there wasn't a single reported glitch of the machines. What was wrong with this stubborn woman? Why couldn't she simply forget, like the rest of them did, and go on with a normal happy life as a perfect citizen?

*

Slava was too late. They let him into the operational room, but Olga was already locked into the Ameliorator and the process of Memory Anaplasty had started. He should have been grateful that the thick oblong tube had a special shield over the patient's head, making it impossible to see their face. There was only a narrow strip of plexiglass above her hands. They'd been washed clean and lay unmoving, the memory rebellion supposedly in the past.

It's better this way, he told himself as he turned to the monitors, looking for any irregularities, but her vitals and neuroscan showed no stark deviations. Of course, he needed to compare her scans before and after the first Memory Anaplasty with this one. But what then? He had years of data – some clearly showed rewiring, others looked the same before, during and after the procedure. Whether it was the soul or some auto-immune response interfering, Slava still could not tell.

Slava remembered Olga's face and the plea. Those arms reaching out – one on her belly, the other as if following an invisible string, blood smeared all over her fingernails. He wondered whether Blinov, with his baby quotas, had ever looked beyond the neat, anaesthetised Caesareans and blissfully unaware faces; whether he'd visited women in the state of Erasure Craze.

Slava suddenly felt feverish and sick. He instructed the neuroplastic surgeon to send him the data when the procedure was done, and then fled before he could receive a reply.

*

The computer screen was showing Slava all the cases of birthing memory resurfacing in the last year on the lefthand side, and the Zero-Interference Birth Group on the right – thousands of scans to be processed to find out what triggered the atavism. He was back to the comforting world of numbers, but they seemed to have acquired a different dimension. Now, when he read the statistics of the Zero Group – the percentage of inherited trauma, psyche instability and disproportionate attachment, the number of cases when mothers refused to let go of the child, the degrees of devastation children experienced after their mother's life was ended (there was a whole table for different age groups) – he could only see the comfort Olga would feel on being reunited with her baby; her peace. His eyes kept picking out the healthy bonds, cases when children developed higher intellect and emotional intelligence. His head buzzed with contradictions.

Slava walked to the window. The view opened into the hospital yard. He began counting the ambulances – most were of the ordinary type, but there was also a batch of orange-lined cars from the Prenatal Facility. The male personnel with special clearance were helping the paramedics to unload the Cuckoo vehicles. Five cars, each with the capacity of three patients. Slava quickly did the calculations – the evening shift would have their hands full. From the fourth floor, the figures on the gurneys looked like oversized dolls. They were all sleeping, giving Slava no clue as to whether they might turn out to be a special case like Olga.

The TV switched on, startling Slava. As the First Channel Logo faded away, the Patriarch appeared on the screen, sitting behind his usual massive redwood desk. The LED-mask that always covered his face was set into a strict yet supportive expression, the tiny pixellated emoji on his temple depicted contentment.

GREAT RUSOVIA CITIZENS, he began his midday address,
ALL IS WELL IN THE COUNTRY.
THE POWER FLOW TO THE DEFLECTOR DOME
HAS BEEN INCREASED GIVING IT EXTRA STABILITY.
IN ADDITION, I AM PLEASED TO ANNOUNCE
ANOTHER BREAKTHROUGH IN GENETIC RESEARCH.
IN THE FUTURE WE WILL OPEN A NEW TYPE OF
HATCHERY
WITH MATRIX MACHINES CAPABLE OF
ENHANCING THE TRANSCRIPTION FACTOR OF
PERFECTION.
THE FINEST IN THE BEST NEW WORLD.

The LED face disappeared from the screen substituted by the general news anchor, who droned on about the most recent productivity statistics. Slava turned back to the window just in time to see the last of the "matrix machines", these "unsuspecting birds", being wheeled inside the building. How much of this genetic breakthrough was real? The transcription factor of perfection sounded like nonsense to him, but, of course, whatever truth there was to it would be classified. Or could this be the Patriarch's reaction to the news of the faulty mothers? What would they do in these new hatcheries? Exploit the Citizen Filament? Perhaps gathering mind scans throughout a person's life wasn't enough, and they'd found a way to ameliorate consciousnesses on the go? He envisaged a neuroplastic surgeon at home as their beeper pinged a departure from the perfect citizen mindstate; the specialist would dive into the consciousness via a remote terminal and reconnect the synapses without the help of an Ameliorator: anxiety, sadness, disturbing thoughts – all gone, bringing perpetuum happiness to the finest of the best new world.

Slava's hand automatically went to his belly button. He had no way of knowing whether he himself was bestowed with the Filament – the information was confidential. Even he, a man of the branch, did not have access to it. For a moment he expected his mind to go blank or a group of men in black to storm into his office. Nothing happened. Slava realised he should be more careful – this Olga case had influenced him too much. Still, he couldn't help but long to understand the why of Olga's case.

*

Seven years later

The Hatchery Maid put the children in pairs and led them through the school gate decorated with balloons and animated plastic cords that kept rearranging themselves in pre-programmed mottos. The colourful spaghetti changed from *Welcome to school!* to *Happy Day of Knowledge!* to *273 is your home now*. Vera came from an advanced hatchery where they taught them to read from the age of three. She was seven now. She liked words, though she had to admit that the stories they were read and allowed to read were like a chicken soup when you took out the onions (she hated those, so that was okay), the carrots (these she could tolerate and she loved their bright colour), the rice (good if not overboiled) and finally the chicken (yummy) to leave just the yellowish transparent liquid. The stories flushed through her mind quickly, leaving her hungry, and she always had a feeling that every character had something missing (like the amputee veterans in the books about the century-old war).

The inner school yard was a huge square, several batches of pupils were already arranged along the three sides of the perimeter. The school building towered over the empty middle. It was a gigantic box of glass panels; the transparent and opaque sections on the side almost made a funny face, while the façade was one huge screen that ran the number 273 in fiery orange, maple leaves cascading down around it.

The Maid led Vera's group to the very front of the right side of the square. They passed the senior pupils on their way, but the older children paid little attention to the novices. At the head of the empty rectangle stood the Teacher – bony with a tight bun on top of her head.

"Handing the Future over into your hands," said the Hatchery Maid, saluting the Teacher. She then stepped aside.

"Taking responsibility for the Future from you," responded the Teacher.

The Maid nodded and left. Vera felt her heart jolt in her chest. The Hatchery, its every nook and cranny, its rules and demands, had become sickeningly common. She craved novelty and change, yet under the strict gaze of their new Responsibility Adult she felt an inexplicable threat.

The Teacher dug her hand into a big satchel resting against her waist and pulled out a thick wad of chevrons.

"Each pair comes to me for the chevron exchange and then proceeds towards the white line over there." She pointed with her chevron stack.

Vera was in the first pair. She and the boy, Misha, walked to the Teacher, who did four quick lacerations on the left shoulder of their jackets so that their old chevrons flaked to the ground. Before Vera knew it, the Teacher had a different device in her hand – a small pistol with a blue rubber sticking out of it. She ran the gun over the place of the old chevrons – it burnt slightly through the fabric – and pressed the new one to what Vera guessed to be glue.

As she went to wait on the white line, she looked down and saw that the new insignia had a QR code, her personal number, the school digits *273* and a holographic emblem of a glasshouse. Her next stage in life had begun.

*

When the speeches were over, a senior pupil walked with a small girl on his shoulder as she rang a bell. Finally, they were all ushered inside the building. At the entrance to their class a woman with a silver face – a robot! Vera realised with excitement – handed her the schoolbag which rattled with writing utensils and notebooks. Her desk was at the very front of the class, a slip with her number glued to the back of the chair and the corner of the table. A large tablet occupied the centre of the desk, embedded in a docking station. It looked similar to the slots the vacuuming robots in the hatchery slept in.

They all took their seats and the teacher stood behind her long table. She pressed something and the screens of their tablets immediately lit with the word DISCIPLINE; at the same time the speakers read it out loud. Then the image changed to show a cartoon – a short smiling man held a pointer and poked it at the frames that appeared one after another.

Correct steps ensure your happiness.

Your teacher has an approved programme for you. Follow it.

Learn by heart your new routine verses.

Contribute to your group and glasshouse. They are your new family.

"What is a family?" asked a girl three rows behind on Vera's left.

"It is a special arrangement that makes up your immediate bond group," replied the Teacher.

Vera frowned. She'd definitely read something different about 'family' in one of the mouldy books from the discarded pile at the back of their Hatchery library. Something about…

"Isn't mother part of the family?" she said.

The Teacher's nose seemed to get sharper and her lips and eyes thinner.

"Where did you hear this word?" her voice was like thunder.

"I… I don't remember."

"Be careful when you listen to the grown-ups speaking," the Teacher continued in the same harsh voice. "They use words that you don't know. Mother is a very technical term. It means a matrix, or a mould. A form to be able to make other things. Perhaps one of the IT people who came to fix your computers in the Hatchery used it."

Vera pretended to be very interested in the short man on the tablet screen who waved his pointer in circles now that all the frames were there. Their Maids, the Operators and the Educator had never allowed them to see people from outside the Hatchery. Did she, too, come from a mould like in those educational films? Or was a mother a person like in that book…?

A weird tingling and sense of cold spread all over her skin, and Vera automatically wrapped her arms around herself. In that mouldy old book, a woman called a mother was hugging a child like that. Maybe, in the old times they called teachers mothers? Vera shot a furtive glance at the Teacher – uptight as she was, Vera couldn't imagine her hugging anybody. Her arms closed tighter around herself.

*

Olga, sitting in the Headmaster's office for her interview, felt anxious. Yet it wasn't even a proper interview – more of an acquaintance meeting. If her CV wasn't good enough, the Bureau wouldn't have sent her to 273.

Olga had been through this process many times in the last seven years because her Rejuvenation Sleep schedule had been increased – they said in her intense line of work they wanted to give her delicate body enough care. They sent her to the Sanatorium every four or five months now. At the beginning she was a bit worried – perhaps she had some strange illness? – but there was nothing out of the ordinary on her medical file.

The employers didn't seem to mind. Some had an opportunity to wait for her return and to cope with existing staff, others received a substitution. In each new school she would always be welcomed identically courteously. Even now the man in his fifties with a dripping moustache smiled at her pleasantly.

"I am sorry you won't be able to do adjustments to today's menu, since all the ingredients have already been delivered, but starting from tomorrow, it's all up to you. I hope you will find your assistant satisfactory. The previous cook was very happy with her. That's before the cook had to go on her second *Rotational FemLeave*." His smile thinned a little. "You'll have all the nine months of her sabbatical to take care of our food."

It made Olga think about her own sole FemLeave seven years ago. The memories of it were very faint for some reason, the joy of them somehow dulled. But Olga guessed that's how time affected people. Or perhaps, it was this nervousness that didn't let her recall the past properly. She had been jittery since the moment she came back from her last trip to the Sanatorium. At first, she thought of telling her doctor, but then she got scared that they would find her at fault and decided to keep quiet.

"Everything all right?" asked the headmaster.

"Yes," Olga said, swallowing hard.

"You've got a perfect record. Our pupils and staff are lucky to have you. But if you need any help throughout the first few days, we are always here for you."

This man was an angel of a headmaster, Olga thought as she stood to leave his office. Still, she couldn't help but look around her apprehensively. Her eyes caught sight of a crumpled missive beneath a large pile of cigarette ash in the rubbish bin. Well, a

Headmaster's job was a stressful one, and she didn't hear about them getting additional periods of Rejuvenation Sleep. (Though she'd known some terrible teachers who'd often been awarded with these bonuses.) He was good not to take it out on his employees.

*

The food in the school canteen tasted much better today – Vera licked the remnants of the creamy beef stroganoff sauce from her spoon and took a sip of her kompot, which was finally sweet, not watery. There was also the smell of rising dough permeating the place. A pirog to go with the afternoon tea after classes would be majestic. Vera hoped it would be a raspberry one.

The first bell sounded, reminding them all that lessons were to resume in five minutes. Her subdermal activated to give her the classroom number and the subject. Vera stood and picked up her tray. Just as she took her place behind a senior boy in a queue for the tray racks, she saw a white uniformed woman gliding behind the window in the wall separating the dining area from the kitchens. The next moment the cook came out. She looked unnaturally thin and uneven, like a dumpling with its filling scraped out. She could use a few slices of pirog herself, Vera thought.

The cook looked at the racks, which were filled almost to the brim, then cast a glance around the canteen in search of a member of the supporting personnel. But there was no adult to help. The boy in front of Vera was tall enough to shove his tray onto one of the top racks, which left only the highest position open for Vera. She rose on tiptoes, but she wasn't even close to reaching it. The cook saw her predicament and leaned forward to take the tray from her. Their hands touched for a brief moment. And Vera suddenly wanted to keep holding that hand – she wanted it glued, magnetized, even sewn to hers.

The tray dropped to the floor, but neither Vera nor the woman seemed to notice. The cook's eyes grew big, her lips moved but the words were silent. Vera felt an odd heat building up in her belly, like a hot water bottle was inside her. She stepped forward and wrapped her arms around the woman's hips, her head landed on the cook's stomach. It felt empty, but something like an echo, different from a normal gurgling of hunger, sounded from inside it. Vera squeezed the woman tighter, though the heat in her stomach was beginning to burn. Slowly, the cook reciprocated.

"My child…" was all she whispered, and Vera thought of the picture from the book that had the word 'mother' in it.

*

Another file landed in Slava's email box. He clicked on the notification immediately and proceeded to peruse it. These days they came from all over Rusovia – his unknown colleagues sending him data on unusual pregnancy consequences. The last warm colours had greyed out of Slava's hair, and his complexion had deteriorated from being constantly shut in his office. He didn't go for the recommended walks, even home – he couldn't miss a single one of those files. The next one for sure must contain the answer, point to the anomaly of the women who refused to forget giving birth. Reveal the soul.

This time, however, it was a child's file from one of Petrograd's schools. For some inexplicable reason, her Citizen Filament had deactivated. Upon extraction it proved to be totally burnt, causing the child some internal damage. Simultaneously, a fresh birthmark had spiralled out of the girl's belly button. To add to his shock there was a note about the woman who had delivered the girl to the hospital. It was said that she refused to allow the girl onto the ambulance unless she was taken on board as well. Her name was Olga Rachmaninova. She kept repeating that the girl was her daughter.

A Peculiar Job – The Wash – Someone Waiting for Me

Liam Hogan

The moment of connection is like opening a door in your brain, a door you didn't know existed. At the flick of a switch you've gone from a dingy studio apartment with a pull-out sofa bed, staring at the grey walls, to a rambling mansion with extensive gardens, a host of conservatories and terraces and even entire floors waiting to be explored. Every room is crowded with strangers, boisterously welcoming you to the—

You yank the skull cap off your newly shaved head and gasp for words. Everyone does, and I smile encouragement and squeeze your arm for reassurance. It's professional rather than genuine, but you don't have time to work that out. Like ninety-five percent of inductees, you're already feeling the keen loss, the claustrophobia of being stuffed back into your single-occupancy box; all that you've known and grown used to your entire life now dull and cramped. With trembling fingers you snatch for the headset, too eager to do anything right.

I help you put it back on, making sure the threadlike wires don't drag as I gather them together. In the moment before your eyes glaze over you thank me, but that's what I'm here for.

There is, according to the latest research, a correlation between those who avoid recreational drugs and those who baulk at HiveTech telepathy. They share a particular set of deeply held, usually unvoiced opinions, as well as certain mental qualities of which low-level autism is just one, fairly frequent, aspect. Asked why they never got round to trying drugs, even as they were being progressively decriminalised, a common answer is one of control. Not a desire for it, but a fear of losing it, and yourself, at the same time. A fear of quick and sudden addiction, not to the supposedly pleasurable rush of endorphin mimicking chemicals, but to a new and uncertain state of mind. It might mean a less anxious, happier person, but will that person still be the *same* person?

You can predict these refuseniks, these telepathic Luddites, with decent accuracy from a short questionnaire. We allocate twice as long for those sessions. Which, and expressly against my nominal job description as someone whose role is to help people connect, I rather look forward to. They're eccentrics, outliers who feel safer in their own skulls, happier in their own heads. Which doesn't mean they're *happy*, far from it. But—

Ah, you're talking now, with the headset back on and your eyes closed. Describing, haltingly, the sensations, the chorus, the symphony of other people's thoughts and feelings. A short-lived phase this, for most.

You do it for my benefit. Trying to share, not yet realising that there are more than a million people that you are already sharing with. And you don't know, can't possibly understand, how hearing even these awkwardly dug out words, these experiences once-removed, makes me feel.

It is a peculiar job I have been recruited to, though I have my own, selfish reasons for accepting it. The official line is that, due to my experience, I have the closest empathy and can best relate to those who are new to all of this. Even if, quite shortly, you'll leave me far behind.

Once you do, you'll have no further need of my ministrations. Headsets malfunction, they need replacing (a nagging worry, that), but you won't need someone to guide you through the initial steps more than once. Don't need someone to quite literally hold your hand, to remind you of your humanity, your individuality.

Even as those things get completely submerged.

The Wash, they call it. It's always loud the first time. Chaotic, to have everyone talking, each over the other. Some of them are angry. Some are sad. Some of them are broken in other ways. There's a subset, much smaller in number than the absent five percent, who are oddly guarded. Though there is no way *not* to think, and every thought can be heard by every other person in the Wash, some watchers slide through the swirling waters and leave little or no wake.

Or so I hear tell. Maybe they're not real, these rumoured ghosts. Merely another conspiracy theory, one of many. Birthed and tainted by a background level of racist xenophobia, an imagined, mysterious cabal with its own nefarious purpose, behind every great leap forward.

A similar conspiracy surrounds HiveTech and the Wash itself, for those yet to take the plunge into its all-engulfing waters. Those who can't afford it. It's not cheap, though getting cheaper. The neural net technology that gave birth to Electronically Assisted Telepathy came completely out of the blue. Side-swiped your Elon Musks and Bill Gateses, rendering them obsolete almost overnight. People talk about it being a gift from aliens – yet another baseless conspiracy – even though the founder of HiveTech is there, in the Wash, the first and foremost of a million minds. But what is one voice among so many? Of no more consequence than yours will be, for all you might dream otherwise.

While the number of plugged-in people is still small, compared to the population of the world, compared to even the population of this country, it is growing steadily. By my own hands at a rate of between fifteen and two dozen people on a good day, and mine is just one of twenty rooms at this clinic. Already there are grumblings within this connected community about the minority that reject it. They say there must be something inherently wrong with those that the Wash cannot absorb, something dark and dangerous that sets them apart, that at the very least they're closed off from intimacy.

But there's no *choice*, in the Wash, about who you are intimate with. There's no filter, no blocking, no invitation-only groups. No privacy. All you can do if it all becomes too much is to remove the headset, and be hit with a sledgehammer dose of FOMO. The newly connected remove them only when they sleep – the constant hubbub can make that tricky until you get used to it. The more experienced leave them on twenty-four-seven. Always on, always connected, always sharing.

Cynically, I wonder if this resentment is buyer's remorse: the generalised feeling by a group of people when an otherwise overlapping group has the temerity to choose a different way of living. Like couples, setting up singletons, confused when their matchmaking fails. Or parents of newborns, gushing about how it'll change their childless friends' lives. How they shouldn't leave it too late, even as they sit, drool-encrusted and giddy at the lack of sleep. Childless friends they'll soon lose touch with; on different paths, like two flashing lights drifting out of sync.

The pressure to conform is building. Telepathy and the group mindset, the Wash, is insanely powerful. Massively disruptive to every industry, including the arts. Some of the writing, the images, the music, to emerge from the Wash is truly revolutionary, unlike anything ever seen before, a quantum leap of hybrid influences, and – so those who are connected claim – we're only seeing the tip of the iceberg, a specially curated portfolio aimed squarely at the unconnected. That most of what is going on in there wouldn't mean anything to those on the drab, dreary outside. That the only way to appreciate it, is to *join*.

All those wonders lie ahead of you. Right now you're an infant, taking your first tentative steps, playing around with different noises without any real understanding of their meaning, trying to fit in with the towering adults around you, far too busy to look at the astounding art on the walls and the stunning sculptures in the niches. But assimilation is impressively swift – how could it not be, with so many teachers on hand?

That will happen after we part, most likely never to cross paths again. My final interaction with this newly inducted member of the Wash is your look of pity when you remember that I am not part of that buzzing crowd of minds, that I have incomprehensibly rejected it. That I'm one of the five percent. I can feel the hardening of my own facial features in response, even as I try to mask my reaction. The blissfully short wrap-up is behind the walls of our differences, and there's nothing I can tell you, as the last of the electronic paperwork is filed, that will have any impact, not even my warning to "be extra careful when crossing the road". At least until you get used to all the distractions.

Sometimes I wonder if I should give the Wash another go. There are benefits that may – *will* – drive people like me into the fold, eventually. I'm aware of them more than most, even more than others of the five percent I work alongside. And perhaps I would try reconnecting, if only I knew how to be one of those mythical watchers. To shut out the most strident of the voices while clinging to my sense of self. To only say what I truly want others to hear. Until then, or until other things transpire, it is a risk too terrible to contemplate. Because no one can keep a secret, not in the Wash.

Away you go, wrapped up and revelling in your growing community, a community which may encompass the whole world before they are done. Certain philanthropists (or is it the Wash, working behind the scenes?) are pushing for the headsets to be made free to those who cannot afford it, even as prices drop and production ramps up. It's not as if HiveTech isn't already insanely rich, it's not as if the Wash doesn't have access to the pooled assets from those wealthy enough to be early adopters. And it's not as if they need to do much in the way of promotion; the cost and the current government regulations are the only things keeping the clinic queues manageable.

The more people who join the crowd, the richer and more powerful the Wash will get, the more people will want, need, to join. The adherents claim that this is at no detriment to the rest of the world, that it's not a zero-sum game. The productivity increase of those who are connected is a bigger leap than that of the industrial or computer revolutions.

I take a drink from my water bottle and check my watch. I've done a dozen connections today, with more scheduled for tomorrow, and more the day after. A waiting list stretching into the indefinite future. It's early yet, plenty of time for at least one, perhaps two more. But I *can't*. I'm frazzled. If I told you I wasn't a people person, I'm guessing you wouldn't be particularly surprised. We five-percenters skew introverted. None of us are naturals at this, but somehow, that helps us in our role; it presents as a vague aloofness, like we're not trying to sell you anything, even if it's really just the perennial difficulty in knowing what to say to those we don't know, those we don't feel entirely comfortable with. Our bedside manner comes across as distracted but benevolent. Like we've done this thousands of times, but still remember what it was like for us.

In reality, the interactions drain our energy, deplete our resources, leave us leaden, even if we do our best not to show it. By the end of the day, or by that mid-afternoon lull, I crave company. The *right* kind. The only kind, for me.

Thankfully my co-workers, my line manager, are understanding. They have their own limits and, despite the ever-present backlog, we're encouraged to listen to our bodies, to our minds, to safeguard our mental wellbeing. To *not* burnout. I might make up the numbers tomorrow. I might not.

It doesn't need someone like me to do this. It could be done by synced up members of the Wash, or even people yet to be connected for the very first time, and there are plenty of *those*. It wouldn't take more than an hour's training and even that might be overkill. But it has been written into the regulations, HiveTech headsets falling under the category of medical interventions. A last ditch attempt by those in power to throttle the roll-out, to slow it down at least a little. There are as yet no politicians who are connected, none who could stand against the charge of not thinking for themselves, but that won't last. Once the connected outnumber the unconnected...

By then, it may not matter. The longer the delay, the more the institutions we are so used to controlling our lives will have become an irrelevance, politicians included. Moving too ponderously, like giant tree-munching dinosaurs, as nimble mammals scamper around and between their clumsy feet.

Except in this particular scenario, every one of those mammals is connected, and, if they so desired, could together bring down pretty much anything they decided to tilt against, from vast corporations to even the largest of governments. The world order is changing and the dinosaurs know it. The trickle will become a flood will become a tidal wave, the Wash sweeping its way across continents.

For the moment, the inductees get us: those who know what connecting feels like, but who aren't connected. As I've said, it's a peculiar job for us to have. Decently paid, even as the mass of people in the Wash are busy rewriting the rules of economics. The job also acts as a kind of defence or camouflage; we are viewed as part of the process, even if we stand to one side. How can we be *anti*, when we're actively helping swell the numbers? And there are other compromises being made. Other reasons to continue doing what I do. Other reasons to resist the Wash a while longer.

By the time I've wiped down the padded chair one last time and made sure the electronic forms have all uploaded to the central server, by the time the room is ready for tomorrow, I'm checking my watch every five seconds. Anxiously playing a game in which *I can't* leave until the minute hand ticks round one more time, however much I want to. When it finally creeps to, and then fractionally past, the hour, I'm as tightly wound as a clockwork toy. I don't linger to chat to my colleagues, and don't meet the eyes of the expectant hopefuls in the waiting room.

I rush on home, along streets in which people are already divided. The ones who wear a headset and the far larger number that don't. The headset wearers congregate in coffee shops and bars shunned by others, because there the clientele doesn't talk, but will all spookily erupt into laughter at the exact same moment. The unconnected stare stupidly into antiquated mobile phones and eye the headsets with envy, unable to comprehend what it is that they are missing out on.

It's a relief to put the key in the lock, to open my front door and step from outside to in, from a world growing stranger every day to one carefully shaped and moulded so that I fit in. So that *we* fit in.

Samuel, my lover, my all, is waiting for me. Meeting me not with a cup of tea, though that will come later, but two headsets and a pat of the couch he's stretched out on. These are not the HiveTech headsets I've spent the day deploying. Those freshly unpacked sets are lighter, sleeker, the wires vanishingly thin. Soon, the engineers say from within the Wash itself, they'll be lighter still, almost invisible, a filigree through which hair can grow.

These two are clunky prototypes and we have seriously voided whatever warranty they might have once come with. They're stolen, and they're hacked. The latter is a bigger crime than the former; hacking HiveTech headsets is strictly illegal. As is the reverse engineering and reprogramming to make them do what we want them to do. What *I* need them to do.

They're a threat, so HiveTech and various governments would have you believe, not only to intellectual property, but to the whole concept of the Wash, to humanity 2.0. A potential weapon of terrorists, of enemy states, of the evil and the desperate – of shadowy elites, the ever lurking watchers, or those like us who dip their toes into the Wash and then recoil, in horror.

They're none of these things, and nor are we. The only difference is that these precious, irreplaceable headsets are tuned to a different channel. A *private* channel.

It is still like throwing open a door in my mind, but to a cosy cottage rather than a sprawling high rise. A comfortable, familiar, somewhat messy detached. Two up, two down; a space for us, just me and my lover. There's no need for conversation, not when we share every thought, every emotion. The tension drifts away with each blissful moment of rapport. There's a surprising amount of catching up to do – all the ideas and discoveries Samuel made through the day, things he would have turned around and excitedly told me had I been there, things that fascinate and delight him, and that he knows will fascinate and delight me. I want to know, first, about the bad stuff, and I breathe an immense sigh of relief when I realise there isn't any, or no more than usual.

I feel fingers – Samuel's fingers, our fingers – gently caressing my cheek, wiping away moisture. It shouldn't be me that is crying, because my dear, sweet lover hasn't been able to speak since cancer ravaged his throat. Despite the rounds of chemo, despite the horrible surgery, despite the ever-present pain that is so immense it has its own room in our cottage, the only one with the door closed, Samuel is in a better mood than I am. He can feel the day lying heavy on me, all these thoughts and worries that have been rattling around my lonely skull, seeking an outlet. Though when they finally find one, they fade away as inconsequential as a tear in a salted sea.

He hugs me, *tight*. I let his love wash over me, and mine over him, and know everything is going to be okay.

The Library is Perfect – An Error – Underwater

Fiona Mossman

The trolley is still mostly full of books but I do not rush. A librarian's work is all about precision, after all: that is how we contribute to the great Library, and there is always shelving to be done.

As I push my trolley up the ramp, I exchange greetings with other librarians, each of us moving at calm, contented paces, applying the correct amount of force to send our trolleys upwards at a steady speed or to prevent them from skiting downwards too fast. "How many books have you shelved since I saw you last?" one asks me with her usual quirked eyebrow and sardonic smile. I grew up with this librarian, before we were librarians, and we received our stacks of books on the same day.

"Two," I announce, halting my trolley as she did the same. "And you?"

"Three," the other librarian says. "I was lucky – two on migrating birds, only one floor apart!"

I smile, gracious. Last time we met, I'd shelved fully four more than she had. It was simply a matter of distance. "Until next time." I nodded to her, and we each continued, one upwards and the other downwards with our precious piles of books. I do enjoy my little rituals with her – we've carried on like that for as long as I can remember.

The Library is perfect. I have travelled many, many leagues in the Library, and I have never found an end to it. Its regularity is exemplary: its knowledge is the sum of everything that can ever be known: every book has its place, as ordained by the Great Beneficent Librarian, and each location in the glorious Classification Scheme has the precise book for each shelf, written in numbers that translate to one of the shelves in one of the rooms of the Library that is the world.

In this scheme, the book is directly equal to the shelf which is directly equal to the subject in all its specificity, set within its divinely correct location in the whole constellation of knowledge. This is the first principle: *Everything has its place.* To find your own place and to stay there, precise and unchanging, is to be perfectly happy, perfectly contained. This is what the Library teaches us.

I reach the floor where the numbers emblazoned across the doorway are a match for the first part of my next book's shelfmark. I enter the doorway and check the shelfmark again, deciphering. I let the numbers lead me through the twists and turns of room after room. I remember when I first started, this was the most difficult part, knowing the layout of the rooms and the pathways by which the shelfmarks dictated your steps: left, right, straight across, left… I used to be so nervous that I would make a mistake! Now my steps are confident and my route unerring, and through each room the signs comfort me: *Room 5736, flowers that grow in acidic soil. Room 5737, flowers that grow in alkaline soil. Room 5738, flowers that grow in mixed soil.* I keep going, through book-lined room after book-lined room.

While we do not read the books, of course, I like to say goodbye to each book as I leave it where it belongs. The book that I have come to this room to shelve is green-backed and handsome, and I flick through its pages, enjoying the illustrations, catching glimpses of its text. I'm admiring a full-colour plate of dainty purple-and-orange petals when I hear a fellow librarian in the corridor and I start guiltily, but they do not look in.

Putting the book back down I begin to count, book by book, shelf by shelf. I am getting closer to the number that represents the final location of the book and the fizz of excitement begins inside me. This is my favourite moment, the moment I locate the correct place. My fingers skim the spines, my lips forming the numbers, each one closer than the next until—

I reach the place but there is something wrong. There is already a book there.

My book, a book on the medicinal properties of pansies, would fit perfectly between the book on the origins of *Viola x wittrockiana* and a slim volume that seems to be a disquisition on the velvety texture of a pansy petal. But instead there is an interloper, snug and smug and completely *wrong*. The shelfmark on the spine doesn't fit the sequence at all. My eyes skip from the code for the shelf to the room code, to the floor code, back through the whole shelfmark in disbelief – the book is not simply a little out of place; it's *whole floors* wrong.

How could this be?

I peer at the spine and read the title: *On Crime*. What is this book doing here, resting in the shelf that is meant for a book on a completely different topic? How could such a catastrophic error have occurred?

My hand is trembling as I do something that I have never done before. I take a book *off* a shelf and put it onto my trolley. Hardly daring to breathe, I pick up the book that it was my task to shelve and I slide it into place. It fits perfectly, the shelfmark label completing the sequence of numbers exactly as it was meant to, and I feel like steel bands have been loosened from my ribcage.

The misshelved book has taken its place on my trolley and it's as if a burning coal sits there, threatening to send everything up in flames. I must get this book to its correct location as quickly as possible, but the whole situation is troubling. The amount of books that I was given to shelve when I first became a librarian was the ideal amount; to add to it is to go against the intentions of the Great Beneficent Librarian. But I cannot do anything else – I cannot leave the book here, for that would ruin everything, the whole perfect system, how things are meant to be.

I wheel my trolley around decisively and begin the long walk back to the ramp. The sooner I shelve it, the better; it's just one detour, then I will be back on track, as if nothing had ever gone wrong. I'll fix it, then I'll get back to what I'm supposed to be doing.

I feel strange. There is a sensation of a blockage, as if there is a tide inside of me and it has come up against a dam. Librarians do not make mistakes; we are trained so rigorously, we each know that what's at stake is nothing less than the order of the whole Library. What child has not run their finger over the tables of the divine Classification Scheme, matching numbers with meanings, marvelling at the absolute correctness of it? What librarian does not march through the rooms of endless books knowing that they have a duty to librarians both past and future, to uphold the Classification? And so how could anyone get this wrong?

Worse, what if it was not an accident? To deliberately misshelve a book – the thought sends a shudder down my spine. To do something like that would be nothing less than an act of mutilation. I cannot credit any librarian with such a deed.

These worries roll around my head to the beat of my feet and the rumble of the castors. I am aware that I am hurrying, my steps occasionally less measured than I know is proper, but this is an emergency and I cannot find it in myself to slow down. There are many rooms still to pass through…

It seems like aeons as I make the long descent to my next designated destination. It's certainly deeper than I have ever been before, and as I go I pass fewer and fewer librarians. I am grateful for this: I do not want them, with their air of calmness and certainty – the absolute happiness that comes with our task, our purpose – to see me this agitated.

At last, the correct floor. I start following the next set of shelfmark numbers. In my haste I make a wrong turn not once but twice, and I have to turn back, palms sweating on the steel handle of my trolley. At least this book is not as deep in, the numbers smaller as the topic is more general.

That sensation of building pressure – a dam in my chest – seems to have returned as I sweep my eyes around the room, looking for the marker from which to begin my count. There is another librarian here, an old man leaning up against his trolley for a break, but I ignore him. There is only one thing that matters right now and I need a clear mind for it. I spot the marker with a surge of glee, and begin the count, letting the soothing tick of numbers be the only thing in my mind.

Just as I am reaching the area of the correct shelfmark I am interrupted.

"Lost, partner?"

I pause with my face pressed up against a book's spine, the divine numbers faltering, scattering at the disturbance. We do not interrupt another librarian's count. Why would anyone do that?

"Did you hear me?" the librarian speaks again.

I whirl around, not hiding my anger. "You made me lose count!"

"Did I now?"

The other librarian does not seem to grasp the significance of this. He examines something under one fingernail, digging at it with another.

"How unfortunate. I do apologise." He doesn't sound very sincere.

"Why, you—"

"I'm merely observing that you seem to be lost. It's a nice state to be in, but you look like you're not the type to get lost much. I thought you would like to know."

I glare at the other librarian. Was there some sort of sick joke going on at my expense? "I assure you," I say with all the haughtiness I can muster, "I am precisely where I mean to be."

The librarian gives a short laugh and crosses the distance between us in a quick, loping stride. Before I can stop him, he swipes the book that I've come here to shelve from my trolley. "Ah," he murmurs as his eyes skim over the long list of numbers, parsing their component meanings. "Of course."

"What?" I demand.

"It's a Classification issue," he says, offering me the book again. I am so taken aback by those words that I simply stare at him as he holds the book between us. "Yes, you heard me," the other librarian says, the corners of his mouth twitching up. "I said that there's an issue with the Classification."

"That cannot be," I say, finally finding my tongue. I snatch the book back. "There are no errors with the shelfmarks. The Classification is perfect."

"Then tell me why a book on crime belongs in the section on medicine."

I look around. The titles of book spines vie for my attention. Medical treatises, books on symptoms, books on cures.

The answer comes to me and as soon as it does I know what is going on. This must be a test! Every librarian must enhance their knowledge by using the perfection of the Library to guide their understanding: and here was a solution, the only logical answer possible. "This book belongs here because to commit a crime is to be sick. Thus we need medicine, for it is every librarian's duty to remain healthy. That is why a book on crime belongs here." Triumphantly, I turn back to the shelves and find the gap where this book belongs. Of course, it slides into the space on the shelf as if the space were made for it: which it was, for this is the Library.

I turn back to the older librarian, ready for praise. But the man has his arms folded and is looking at me with an expression that I cannot quite decipher. "Ah, child," he says with a sigh. He taps the title, drawing my eyes back to the book that I have just shelved. "Do you not think there is another place that this book could belong? Have you not passed a section related to social organisation? Was there not a room on justice? A room for each type of crime that exists?"

I frown. There were such rooms; I had shelved a book on that floor years ago. "You're talking nonsense," I told him. "A book can only have one shelfmark. *This* is where it is meant to be. Another place – *fah!* That's like saying a person can be two people at once."

The man's smile deepens. "Let me ask: what was the book you shelved before this?"

"It was a book on the medical uses of pansies. Shelfmark 2429.5789.1232."

The man tilts his head to one side as if making a calculation. "Follow me," he says.

"I've wasted enough time—"

"Just come," he repeats, pushing his trolley out of the room. I can hear the squeak of one unoiled castor as he disappears, repeating each time the wheel rotates. I find myself following the sound, deeper and deeper into the network of rooms. My own well-oiled trolley glides noiselessly between us.

The librarian hums to himself as he takes turn after turn, checking his progress against the signs on each entranceway. At one point I see him leaning on the trolley so that his feet glide above the floor, like a child, not a librarian. Despite all of my confusion and the heavy feeling in my chest, this is oddly uplifting. Eventually we reach a room where the librarian turns towards the shelves, running gnarled fingers along spines until he finds what he's looking for. A green-backed book is slid out from its snug location and handed to me.

I recognise this. It's the book on the medicinal uses of pansies, the one I shelved earlier, many floors above this.

"No," I say. I flick open the pages, glimpsing the illustrations, just as they were in that other book. "It must be a different one."

"Must it?"

"The same book on two different shelves? On different *floors*? That's…"

"Unthinkable," the other librarian says, his gimlet eyes on mine. "And yet."

My eyes are drawn to a colour plate, the purples and oranges of the petals clustered in such pleasing shapes. It's the same. Could he have moved it, somehow? Changed the shelfmark? No; I must be mistaken; there are lots of books, after all. This is not that one.

Yet the subject, at least, remains the same – so how can the system be absolute…?

"Ask yourself this question," the librarian says, his soft voice cutting through my turbulent thoughts. "What does this book actually refer to? What actually is a pansy? Are there any in the Library?"

"No, of course not," I say, confused all over again.

"Wouldn't you like to see one?"

"I don't understand."

"Wouldn't you like to see a pansy? What this book is talking about?"

"There are no pansies in the Library…"

"Then how can there be a book about their medicinal properties?"

I shove the book back into its place and step away from it, from him, putting my trolley between us. I don't understand anything, my head is spinning, and all I need is to get away. Without another word, I turn and flee.

That man must be sick. That must be why he is down there. He's sick, and he was trying to infect me too. I should warn someone. That's what a responsible librarian would do.

But first, I need to rest. I feel worn, like trolley wheels after decades of spinning. I decide to head to the rooms where the beds are kept, laid out in neat rows for librarians to use at need. I'll file a report when I wake up.

*

Dreams trouble my sleep, images of pansies curling towards each other like conspirators and footsteps hurrying down corridors that lead nowhere. These visions are more signs of the sickness that seems to be spreading into me, and yet, when I awake, I do not report the old man nor visit an apothecary-librarian. My brain must have simply been overheating; it's natural, when you go that far down in the Library. Now that I'm back at the usual floors, I'll be able to work again. That's all I want to do.

Yet I feel as if I am two people. One part of me pushes the trolley, marching steadily with the others up the ramp on my way to my next shelfmark. The other part remains with the dreams: purple and orange, a throbbing hum, a softness – a weakness – deliciously spreading through my body…

"Are you alright?"

It's my old friend, the librarian I grew up with. She's staring at me as I drag my fractured selves back together, blinking as if there is too much light here when it's the same as it ever was. "I forgot…"

"Yes?"

"I forgot… where I was going."

She stares at me, concern etching her features. She looks at one of the books on my trolley. "What! You've gone too far," she says. "You came from level 25021, right? You're five floors past this shelfmark!"

I look where her finger is pointing. The numbers, which previously marched upwards with comforting regularity, drift before my eyes, unmoored. But she's right. I've gone past the floor.

"Here," she says. "I'll come with you."

She turns my trolley smartly with one hand, setting it alongside hers. Together we begin the descent, and she only lets go of the handle of my trolley when she sees that I am controlling it.

We head into the entranceway five floors down, our steps falling into a rhythm. Her presence at my side feels at once safe and incredibly dangerous. This is my old friend; she knows me – but what would she say if I told her about the strange things that are happening to me? The thoughts that I cannot seem to control – about whether there is an end to the Library, about books being in multiple places… And why have I never noticed before, that the way her hair falls around her face – asymmetric yet somehow still beautiful – makes me want to brush it from her eyes?

She catches me looking at her. "What?" She's only half paying attention, her gaze focussed on the room numbers, guiding us towards my next shelf. She doesn't need to be doing this.

I glance around. There are no other librarians here. "Have you…"

"Have I what?"

I swallow to moisten a suddenly dry throat. "Have you ever seen… a flower?"

Her trolley squeaks in protest as she comes to an abrupt stop. I stop beside her and I cannot seem to pull my eyes up from the floor to see the expression on her face.

When she finally speaks – aeons have passed while I've waited, I'm sure – it's in a soft tone, almost missable. "Aha," she says. I look up. She's smiling.

Moving slowly, deliberately, as if not to startle a wild animal, she leans over and plucks a book from my trolley. She turns it over gently in her hands, considering. Then she goes to the nearest bay and slots it in on a shelf near head height, pushing it flush with an exact and gentle push of her fingers.

The shelfmark is entirely wrong, but the book sits there, inconspicuous and innocent. My eyes are fastened to her, iron to a magnet, as the thoughts whirl and crash around my head.

It was her. She has been misshelving.

My two selves are splitting, splintering, smashing – and there is a thrill building inside me, a reckless, giddy abandon.

"You've been reading," she says softly, and it's not an accusation, though it's hard not to hear it as such.

"I want to know about pansies," I say. Velvet petals, purple, orange, blooms that burst – does it hurt, when a flower blooms?

"There is only the Library. The Library is the world."

"But then… how can there be books about pansies?"

She nods. "Somewhere outside the Library, there must be pansies."

"Yes."

We don't have to speak – anything else we could say is already understood. The Library is not perfect; the Classification obscures, even as it reveals. And she knows it too. She's been trying to show me. She's looking at me in that way she always does – our little competitions, our little conspiracies, a quirked eyebrow and a sardonic smile – and I know that I can never unlearn what I know now. That I do not want to.

The sweetness of it washes over me. The dam has burst and I am underwater, but I've never seen so clearly.

All of the possibilities are unfolding: books slipping from their assigned places, librarians on their trolleys sliding down the spiral ramp with childish glee, and the world beyond the totalising walls of the Library, the world where I know there must be flowers that push their way through dark soil and burst their blooms, bright purple, bright orange. All this and more I know as I take her hand and brush the hair from her eyes.

Education – The Final Ingredient –
The Cost of Living

Ian Whates

Meredith frowned, not happy with the state of the kilterwheat crop.

The readings all appeared to be normal. Humidity, temperature, luminosity, soil composition… everything seemed to be exactly as it ought to be, gauged to ensure optimal growing conditions for kilterwheat within the Dome. Yet the plants' leaves lacked a degree of lustre to her critical eye. It was nothing obvious and the difference so slight that she couldn't be certain, but experience had taught her to trust her instincts, and those instincts were troubled.

She double checked and then triple checked the settings. The ambient solar lamps were mimicking the sun's radiation perfectly, at this stage in the wheat's development providing a little under eight hours of uninterrupted sunlight per day. Temperature sat comfortably in the middle of the 20 to 24° C optimum range, and a quick glance through recent records showed no deviation beyond those parameters. The sprinkler system delivered carefully governed levels of rainfall – a total of 35 cm would fall across the growing season. The soil in which the crop grew remained as it should be – loamy, low in iron, sodium and magnesium, whilst drainage was good and salinity levels sat well within acceptable limits… Every reading indicated this to be a healthy crop.

So what exactly was it that niggled at her?

The lunch beep sounded while she was still trying to analyse her disquiet – not a claxon, just a gentle beep, all that was needed within the quiet ambience of the Dome. Dutifully, she took her sandwich packet and made her way to the rec area. After taking her usual seat, she looked up to see her regular lunchtime companion, Karen, approaching. The two exchanged smiles by way of greeting as Karen sat down, and they opened their sandwiches together. Today it was yeast extract in kilterwheat bread that awaited them within the seaweed packaging, the rich almost meaty scent of the filling causing Meredith to realise, with some surprise, just how hungry she was.

"So, how're things at the beating heart of the Dome?" Karen asked around a mouthful of sandwich.

"Well…" and Meredith shared her concerns.

Once she had finished, Karen asked, "Have you passed any of this up the line?"

"Of course not." *And say what, exactly?* she wondered.

"Good. Don't. They won't do anything about it and will just mark you down as a trouble maker."

They each chomped down another bite before Karen said, "How much do you know about farming, its history I mean?"

Meredith pondered that for a second. "Well, I know the domes were established by the State after they overthrew the corrupt Parliament and liberated the populace—"

"Yes, yes, we all know that," Karen interrupted, "but I mean *before* that, before State standardised production and brought all the agriculture into the domes."

Meredith realised she had only the vaguest idea of what had come before that. "Disorganised… haphazard growing of food crops for individual profit rather than the benefit of us all," she ventured.

Karen grunted. "In a way," she said, popping a final bit of sandwich into her mouth. "You see, farming used to be a way of life. Not some scientifically monitored process carried out in controlled environments by functionaries like you and me – no offence intended – but a vocation, one pursued by people who cared about the land they worked, who understood the environment. They made sacrifices, investing blood, sweat and tears into growing and harvesting their crop in the face of unpredictable weather and changing seasons…" She screwed up the seaweed packaging and dropped it into the recycle chute beside the seat. "If you're right and the kilterwheat *is* in the early stages of ailing, I doubt it's the nutrients or supplements that are wrong – they'll be perfectly balanced as always – it's the human connection, that's the missing ingredient.

"Anyway, that's what I reckon." So saying, she stood up and headed off. "See you tomorrow."

*

Lunch finished, Meredith went back to her workstation. Karen had given her much to think on, and she mulled it over, trying to see how her friend's theory might fit around her own disquiet, which showed no sign of abating. She stared at her screens for a moment, concluding there was little point in going over the same old ground for a fourth or even fifth time, so instead she settled on a more hands-on approach.

Grabbing her spray bottle and soil sample kit, she made her way down to the crop level.

The vast field of wheat stretched into the distance before her as far as the eye could see. She crossed to the nearest plant, which rose high and proud, its crown as tall as she was, and sprayed a fine mist of water from the bottle, watching as the droplets settled on the leaves, lending them for an instant a deeper, richer lustre; but still not rich enough.

Next she knelt down and placed the business end of the soil probe flat to the ground, a respectful distance from the kilterwheat so as not to risk disturbing the roots, and triggered it. A gentle vibration indicated that the probe had done its work, and she returned probe and sample to the kit bag.

In theory, analysing this plug of earth should tell her no more than the instruments had, but she had to try *something*.

It was while she was stowing away the probe that she heard the voices. Children's voices.

She whipped her head around and looked up. There they were, on the viewing gantry. More than a dozen little people in homogenised grey-blue uniform, and two adults; one a woman – presumably their Educator – and the other Mr Williams, the Farm Manager.

The tour! In her preoccupation with the kilterwheat's health, she had completely forgotten about the tour.

"As you can see," Williams was saying, his voice booming out, "here at Peoplesdome Farm we take our work very seriously." Meredith snorted, glad she was too far away for the sound to carry to those in the gallery, for all that it had excellent acoustics. *Nobody* called this place 'Peoplesdome Farm', apart from Mr Williams, but then he was the Manager. To everyone else it was simply 'the Dome'.

"Below us," Williams continued, "you can see Meredith, one of our Crop Overseers, inspecting the kilterwheat in situ, though I'm sure she'll be joining us shortly."

The last was said sharply, and Meredith heard in his tone the unspoken *Get up here now!* She hurried to comply.

She hated these school visits, which were supposed to be educational, intended to enable the children of the Urban Elite to discover how the food they took so much for granted was grown and developed. In fact, it was little more than an opportunity for the City snobastards to reaffirm their sense of superiority by lording it over the poor country yokels like her. It was rare indeed to find an Elite child who had the faintest interest in the process of farming; all they were concerned with was that the end product should be on their plates when necessary.

They came here to scorn, not to learn, and given the choice no doubt each and every one of them would rather be somewhere other than 'Peoplesdome Farm', most likely somewhere reality was either augmented or virtual.

Meredith took great care to show none of this as she approached the cluster of Elites, marshalling her thoughts and composing her features into a welcoming smile.

"Ah, Meredith, good of you to join us," said Williams. "Everything is well with the crop, I take it."

"Of course," Meredith assured him, anticipating a reprimand once the tour was over for not being here to greet the snobastards when they arrived.

She then turned her attention to the children in question and slipped into the familiar spiel. "Welcome to the place where magic happens and food is grown…" As she spoke, her mind on automatic having given this speech so many times before, she assessed her audience. They were like all the others: bored, most not even bothering to hide their disinterest.

"Who here has ever seen a living plant before?" A flicker of interest from one or two but no reaction from the majority. She wondered how many were wearing earbuddies and not even listening to her. "Well," she persisted, "today you're going to get the chance to stand right next to the crop and touch a kilterwheat stalk. Imagine that, a living, growing plant…"

"Yuck!" said one of the girls. "You mean go down there," and she pointed towards the sea of wheat below them. "In the *mud?*"

At last, a reaction; at least this one was listening.

"It's not mud…" Meredith began, but the girl had already looked away and now produced a flickerstick from her pocket, a device capable of conjuring multiple entertainments, some of which could prove detrimental to the Dome's carefully modulated environment.

"Please put that away," Meredith said, more sharply than intended.

Sharp enough to draw Mr Williams from his conversation with the Educator, evidently. He stared at her in startled fashion, a look that quickly transformed into a thunderous glare.

"Flickersticks are not permitted here," Meredith ploughed on, reckoning Williams' glare would turn even darker if the device did anything to interfere with the conditions in the Dome and affect the crop. Rules were there for a reason and no one, not even an Elite snobastard, was above them. She looked across to the Educator, seeking some support. It was the woman's job, after all.

The Educator: slender, smartly dressed, elegantly poised and innately stylish – in short everything Williams aspired to be but would never achieve – roused herself sufficiently to say distractedly, "Oh do put it away, Veronica."

The device disappeared, though not without a sour furrowing

of the girl's brow and a daggered look cast in Meredith's direction. The poison in that glare brought home to Meredith the danger in the social gulf that existed between her and this 'Veronica'. The consequences should the girl choose to log a complaint against her didn't bear thinking about, and she really *needed* this job, but just at that moment she didn't give a damn.

"Let's take a look at the soil enricher now, shall we?" said Williams, perhaps seeing the malice on Veronica's face or perhaps simply seeking to move the class away from Meredith's influence as soon as possible.

Whatever the reason, she wasn't about to complain at her part in the pantomime being cut short, breathing a sigh of relief as the grey-blue gaggle were escorted the short distance along the gantry to where a large copper tank stood. A broad pipe emerged from the top of the tank to disappear through the floor of the level above, and she knew that a similar pipe emerged from its base, continuing down to crop level and then beneath the loam.

This tank and others like it, set at intervals around the Dome, were where the minerals and supplements necessary to maintain optimum soil conditions were formulated and mixed, raw materials broken down and blended before being distributed by underground feeds throughout the kilterwheat field.

A gentle bass thrum accompanied by a row of brightly lit red and green lights on the tank's hull indicated that a new cycle was underway, the enricher active. For an instant, she and Zane – the technician waiting by the tank to greet the class – exchanged a sympathetic glance of sufferance over the children's heads, then he started his introduction.

Now that she had passed the snobastards onto the next section there was no reason for Meredith to hang around; by rights she should have returned to her workstation, but she didn't. Afterwards, she couldn't have said why, but some instinct kept her there. So she saw the schoolgirl – Veronica – step forward, and heard the high clear voice cut through Zane's words like a knife through butter, interrupting his explanation of the enrichment process.

"I wish to see inside it." Imperious, confident that no one would refuse her.

Zane's voice faltered. He gaped at the diminutive yet commanding figure. "I… the enricher is active," he gabbled. "We can't open—"

"I wish to see inside it," Veronica said again, louder. "Now!"

"Yeah, this is boring," one of the others piped up – a boy. "Just a big metal drum that's sitting there. Show us something that's actually *doing* something."

"Perhaps an inspection hatch…?" Williams piped up, presumably remembering that he was supposed to be in charge here. "Something that can be opened without interrupting the enrichment cycle."

There he went again, showing his ignorance. Once underway the cycle *couldn't* be interrupted, not without wrecking the equipment and jeopardising the Dome's crop.

"It's too dangerous," Zane insisted. "The forces…"

"There *is* such a hatch, though, correct?" the Educator said.

Zane nodded mutely.

"Then open it," she said. "Whatever your fears, I assure you it can't be as dangerous as my wards reporting their dissatisfaction to their parents following this visit."

Zane looked helplessly towards Williams, who waved impatiently for him to continue.

With a defeated air, Zane pressed a button and an oblong section of the tank's copper housing protruded forwards before sliding to one side. It wasn't a huge section, but what it revealed was chaos, and the previous thrumming noise escalated to a muted but incessant roar. This was the first time Meredith had seen the process directly, and she was finding the downward jet of multi-coloured materials mesmerising, the speed of its passing hard to process. As one, the children surged forwards for a closer look.

"No, stay back!" Zane tried to block them but was swept away by their charge.

What came next happened so quickly it was all a bit of a blur, which Meredith could only make full sense of later, when she had a chance to analyse events properly. She saw Veronica holding her flickerstick towards the open hatch, presumably intending to record the nutrient stream – nor was she the only one now holding such a device. The flickerstick was wrenched from her hand by the wake of the flow, or perhaps she simply dropped it. Either way, the stick disappeared through the hatch.

With a scream of denial, Veronica lunged forward in an attempt to catch it, only to fall or be dragged through the hatch herself. She was gone in the blink of an eye.

Instantly, the chit-chattering children fell silent, too shocked to move or even give voice. The only sound was the relentless threshing of the enricher as it continued its work, though Meredith fancied she detected a subtle change in its timbre; there seemed to be a new rhythm buried deep within its roar, a steady pulse like a distant heartbeat.

Zane was the first to react, stepping across to press the button and close the hatch. This acted as the release they all needed and suddenly they could all breathe again.

"Stop the enricher!" Williams commanded, a little hysterically.

"We can't," Zane told him. "Once it's underway the cycle has to run its course. We *can't* interrupt. She's gone."

The Educator had visibly wilted. Hands pressed to her cheeks, she looked on the verge of fainting. "What… what am I going to tell her mother?"

"We'll have to destroy the entire crop in this section of the field," Williams muttered.

They wouldn't, Meredith knew that. State would never countenance such a financial loss.

Whatever imperative had held her here was gone, releasing its hold, allowing her to slip away and return to her workstation. There were plenty of folk on hand to deal with the aftermath of the accident; that wasn't Meredith's department.

Karen's lunchtime revelations came back to her, with certain words leaping to the fore: '*sacrifice… blood… the human connection*'. Her disquiet regarding the health of the kilterwheat, which had troubled her all day, had finally vanished. She knew beyond doubt that the next harvest would be a bumper one.

Art-crime – Artifacts – Age of Birds

Michael Teasdale

Thought-log #4327

Perhaps the most troubling thing about the vandals is their lack of a clear motivation. We have a saying in the department: that to understand the motivation is to gain a foothold in the solution. Yet, here we are, weeks removed from the appearance of that first abomination, scrambling for certainty and with a lack of traction that is as notable as it is regrettable.

The disturbance to the public is deliberate; of that much we are sure. The devious machinations of the Second States in attempting to lower worker productivity and set back the war effort are obvious, and yet…

Why this particular blasphemy?

Why a bird?

Perhaps the image chosen was random. After all, the rendering of a crow, daubed in black tar was technically a crime on four different fronts.

The first could be seen as a minor misdemeanour; the wasting of a public resource, the tar having been set aside for other purposes.

The second crime, however, the defacement of a government building, carries a penalty that is justifiably harsher.

The third crime, wilful engagement in public distraction, can be regarded as little short of treasonous, given the current political climate.

As for the fourth crime: the use of an unsanctioned image. It is so unheard of in this day and age, that public memory can scarcely recall the last major offence to take place. I refer of course to what was once labelled an 'art-crime', before such criminality became so uncommon that its usage almost disappeared from our everyday lexicon.

In truth, there hasn't been a recorded art-crime in over a century and the laws that covered the sanctioning of imagery roll back even further than that to the very founding of the Ministry of Public Images.

It made sense that the Ministry's own building was chosen as the target for this crude daubing. While the hosing and subsequent removal of the offending visual made for a most satisfying public spectacle, this was, arguably, a further distraction from the daily routine of our citizens; most of whom should, by their timetable, have been partaking in daily exercise instead of gathering to cheer on the heroic firefighters as they hosed the tar feathers away.

While the raucous public approval that met this intervention was a validation of the unity of our system, it has not erased the lingering doubt that the daubing of the image set festering in the minds of the public. The very idea that the mental illness that once led citizens to call themselves 'artists' has returned to sully the purity of our society remains a terrifying thought. Perhaps then, the people needed to see it washed away by the fire department's hoses. Yes... the more I think about it, the better it was for them to have witnessed it; a regrettable, but failed, attempt by insurgents of the Second States to uproot the order we have worked so hard to achieve.

Still, I cannot help wonder... why a bird? What could it mean?

Such contemplation is, of course, a planned part of the attack. This is the danger of unsanctioned imagery. Like the religions of days gone by, such unapproved design might lead a troubled mind on a journey that could detract from the purity of routine that our social structure has perfected.

The Ministry of Public Images is here to keep us safe. They provide all of the properly explained visual stimuli our society could ever need. All of it vetted and approved for its clarity and transparency. We revel in the completeness of these images. Why, even here, in my office, I have hanging behind my desk one of my favourite sanctioned images. It depicts a pink isosceles triangle pointing upwards, hovering above a vertically elongated green rectangle. This, of course, is image #234, one of the most famous visual motifs released by the Ministry over the last fifty years. It represents the rocket we intercepted prior to the founding of The Party. The blessed gift from the stars that first brought the sacred teachings to our world. There is absolutely no room for interpretation with image #234, which is the wonderful thing about officially sanctioned images. They can be consumed by a citizen, bring about the required edification, and then be cast aside for more important matters without troubling the brain with unproductive inference. Not a second is wasted pondering their significance as each comes complete with its own detailed user guide, providing not only a complete explanation of the image in question but guidance on how and where the imagery can be displayed and the context it is applicable within.

Behold the pink triangle as it hovers above the green rectangle!

There is absolutely no doubt that the image is that of a rocket.

It can only be a rocket.

Nothing else.

Yet, why does my mind turn to my cabinet drawer?

Thought-log #4328

Two weeks after the removal of the crow, the disturbing image had almost left our minds.

This was when the second art-crime appeared. After the first incident, no tar barrel was left unattended, yet the vandals found a new method to complete their illegal design. This time, a chalk-like substance, for marking the space where the road was to be realigned, had been used to scratch out the image of a dove across the redbrick wall of offices of the Ministry for Peacetime Preservation.

The embarrassment to the Ministry was absolute and the effect on morale was obvious. This assault on the eyes was almost certainly chosen to coincide with the much-publicised recruitment drive, and barriers had to be quickly erected to divert these young citizens to a rear entrance in order to avoid exposing them to this scandalous defacement.

I was sent by the department to supervise the scene as, for the second time, the Firefighters turned their hoses on something other than a blaze.

I will admit that I've begun to fear for these brave public servants as the art-crimes have increased. Their continued exposure to these unauthorised images, without the high-level training of agents such as myself, must be damaging to their unprepared psyches. I have considered recommending to my superior that their squadrons be rotated to minimise the effect but, of course, this would imply that the vandalization will continue, that the images cannot be stopped, that the only solution to the problem is to clean and clean again.

This is a prediction I do not feel comfortable delivering.

In any case. There is now more to consider. Something more troubling has occurred. The vandals have begun to do more than simply daub their blasphemies. Now they leave behind the tools of their trade for others. They are actively and surreptitiously recruiting.

We cannot be certain if they left similar artifacts at the scene of the first abomination. A search has been conducted, but I cannot shake the feeling we were too late.

The banned artifacts were easy to miss. Laid out for more curious citizens to find in the nearby gutter or hidden among cracks in the wall. Presumably even left behind for the Ministry's own new recruits to stumble upon as they entered or exited the building.

At first, we thought they were primeval weapons of a kind; tiny sharpened sticks that might make for neat assassination tools by the primitives we are at war with.

I held one in my hand as I supervised the latest cleaning. A cylinder with a sharp pointed end. Foolishly, as if my own brain had been corrupted by what I'd seen, I found myself unable to resist pressing it against the end of my finger and was horrified to see it leave behind a mark. Concerned that this may be some type of trace poison, I returned in haste to the medical unit of the department, where the nurse was able to assure me that it was nothing more than leftover residue from the mineral graphite.

Bagging the item for evidence I took it for analysis to the Department of Historical Artifacts where its true nature was ultimately revealed to me.

It was what, in pre-enlightenment times, people called a 'pencil'. A crude tool used to scratch out words on paper. Of course, words were not the vandal's intention here. Oh no! The pencil was also once a popular tool in the hands of the mentally insane. The citizens who called themselves 'artists' and who would commit their madness to paper with the absolute intention of causing confusion, puzzlement and, in extreme cases, philosophical doubt in the minds of citizens whose grasp on order and structure was already tenuous in the days before the Great Awakening.

Put simply, had these tools fallen into the hands of ordinary citizens then all manner of unlicensed imagery might have sprung forth as a result. The disruption would be intolerable. Imagine it! Our perfect orderly society once more consumed by anxiety, uncertainty and chaos. It is the dream of our enemies in the Second States. They hate us for our stability and will do anything to sabotage it. We must not allow them to succeed.

When I returned to the complex, I could still sense the strange mark on my finger, even though I had scrubbed it away entirely. It reconfirmed to me just how dangerous even the smallest exposure to an unlicensed image can be.

I spent some time in my office that evening, staring at the purity of image #234, letting the comforting regularity of its rectangular body wash over me, gazing with solemn understanding at the sharp rising point of the triangle at its tip.

It was, as ever, the perfect, tranquil image of a rocket.

By the time I was finished with my meditation, I could barely recall what the 'pencil' even looked like.

Thought-log #4329

I do not know why I took one home.

I have considered that, perhaps, my theory about the dangers posed to the poor, unknowing firefighters by their repeated exposure to these images may be more pressing than I imagined.

The images, always of birds, have now appeared in

multitudes too serious to simply label them the work of a lone insurgent or even a small fraction of our increasingly politically disaffected youth.

Clearly, it is no longer a matter of distraction but one of mass subversion. Art-crime is now a serious problem and illegal artifacts are being recovered on a daily basis, no longer limited to those lying scattered at the scene of a crime.

Where once I would not have dared to take one for private study, so many are now being bagged and evidenced that the act of slipping a pencil into my lapel pocket was not a difficult one. Aside from pencils, crude implements of wood and horsehair known as 'brushes' have been retrieved from the homes of suspected subversives. These allow the quick spreading of liquid pigments that can be mixed to form rudimentary colours to produce what was once knows as 'paint'. This 'painting' can recall almost any aspect of the avian life that, over a century ago, could still be seen within our city walls but which are, like other carriers of infection, now found only in the disease-ridden Second States.

At this point the pencils are almost considered a minor threat in comparison to these larger tools and yet the internal anguish I feel at having smuggled one away is all-consuming. I have taken it out from my desk drawer several times to look at it. There is something about the precise mechanics of its design that seems to set it aside from other artifacts and now I think I see just what that is. The long thin body is red, not green, the tip browner than the pink I am accustomed to, but, other than that, the comparison is clear. It has corrupted me. Of that I am sure. I can no longer look at image #234 and see only a rocket.

Now a pencil stares back at me.

And what greater problem does this then evidence? That the Ministry of Public Images is fallible? That they have allowed onto the streets an image of potential subversion, an impure depiction that can, with the right knowledge, be interpreted as something other than its intended design?

A further, far more disturbing thought occurs to me. That this is not some happy accident. That the Ministry of Public Images itself has fallen victim to the corruption long ago. That image #234 was never intended to portray the rocket, but was always intended to portray the pencil. That the official interpretation was only ever accepted for so long due to the vast majority of citizens never having seen or heard of the latter.

What now then? How many others have gone home after gazing upon a scrawled abomination, hoping to seek absolution in an image such as #234 and instead finding only the same internal confusion as I myself have suffered?

Worse is the compulsion I now find myself gripped with. An obligation to amend the sacred image. An image which I once saw as pure rocket. Only rocket. Nothing else. Now it seems incomplete. My mind screams to me to take the pencil from my desk drawer and use it, to commit not only art-crime but also thought-crime. To take the pencil and darken the tip of the rocket, to overlap its wonderful pink triangle with a smaller darker triangle. To turn an instrument of order into an instrument of chaos. To turn the rocket into a pencil. To turn a sacred image into 'art'.

The pull is so strong. And the thrill, the thrill I feel...

It is a strange kind of freedom.

Thought-log #4330

They will come for me. Of that I am certain. It no longer matters anymore. As I look out across the once orderly city, I see that I am not alone in my sick criminality.

We are as one, in our own way; we mentally insane. We artists.

I smuggled home my first brush earlier in the month, long after I first altered what I once referred to as image #234. The thrill of defacing it seems so minor now, given all I have done since. The sketches I have made, the drawings that serve no purpose, the strange paintings I have spent evenings busying myself with, mixing together household components to make my wicked paint. I have even begun using the pencils to write these words, in the crazed manner that scribes once did before automatic thought-logs were first introduced.

Earlier today I climbed to the roof of my complex and, with stolen brush in hand, announced publicly both my guilt and my surrender to the authorities. Yet, above all, I have announced something greater:

My dissent.

With the crumbling of my belief in image #234, I renounced my faith in The Party and the beliefs that I once held to be undeniable. The bird I chose to paint reflects the path I have chosen. A magpie. Its black and white wings now daubed across the rooftop of my complex for all to see. Magpies, I have learned, were seen as birds of ill omen but also, like myself, they are thrifty thieves. In the Department of Historical Artifacts I found that rhymes were once sung about magpies. According to one such rhyme, nineteen of them were thought to represent safety from a crime. Alas, the paint I was able to procure left only room for one.

One, I learned, was for sorrow.

Yet it is not sorrow I feel as I await my inevitable arrest and the public trial and sentence that will follow.

From high up here, I look out across the city and see that I am part of a flock of resistance. On a nearby complex, a giant albatross has been painted across the glass of a skylight. Close by, I see an unknown figure, busying themself with the portrait of a phoenix daubed in fiery red.

The interpretation of the latter is so clear it could almost have come from the Ministry itself. Yet, these are but two of the wonderful, unauthorised images that continue to appear daily as our citizens' Second Awakening begins.

We have been sleepwalking for so long. It was a wonderful, orderly dream but now we have awakened into the bright chaos of the knowledge that our world was a lie. Everything will be questioned once the veil is fully lifted. The war. The rocket. The nature of The Party itself.

We have the images to thank for this and to remind us never to drift back into slumber. This wonderful avian army exists like the birds outside our cursed dome, freeing our thoughts and minds.

Interpret them how you will, dear reader.

They can be nothing and anything and everything all at once. They belong to no one and everyone and that is their horror and that is their triumph.

The Age of Order is nearing its end.

We rise like the phoenix through the chaos and the fire that will soon follow, soaring, with renewed purpose into the Age of Birds.

Anatomy of Emotion –
The Carving of Chance – Seize the Moon

Ana Sun

Anger in the body: a coiled snake, a raging wildfire.

Anxiety in the gut: the doom-laden twist of a strangler fig.

Em – I definitely wasn't angry at her. If anything, my anger was reserved for myself: me, and my own cowardice.

I ran my thumb around the twenty-sided die in my palm, feeling its precise triangles, its edges sharp enough to carve chance into defined probabilities – just not quite sharp enough to mark my skin.

Swirling it thrice, I let the die drop soundlessly on the grass beside me. It rolled off the hem of my skirt, then a little way down the hillside I was sitting on, settling between a cluster of clover and a young sprout of chamomile. The white numeral on its topmost face glistened in the late afternoon light, picking up a tinge of orange from the departing sun.

Fifteen. *Sit and breathe awhile.*

I must have been nine or ten years old when I'd found an entry in our Chronicles describing an old tradition of using randomness. A list of actions matched up to numbers on a set of dice or a shuffled card deck, an aid for moments of hesitation. I had no idea what the cards looked like, but shortly after that, I found a schema of a die – so I crafted my own.

Pulling a breath deep into my lungs, I willed the anger inside to dissipate, the anxiety to dissolve. Anger about something or someone had a semblance of shape. Anger at myself? A formless force, a relentless riptide.

Letting go of this might take a long time, if ever.

Under the shadow of the old elm tree, the earth seeped cool, the meadow still damp from last night's rain. From the edge of the foothill below, an eclectic mix of coloured tents with no uniformity in size or structure spread across the plain – our summer settlement, most of which would be gone by the end of tomorrow.

A gaping hole in the middle had appeared since yesterday; some of the tents had been moved outwards to make room for tonight's festival. For days now, all of us had brought masses of kindling and dead wood for the bonfire. Around the clearing, movement rippled: a few tall youths hoisting up strings of solar lights, others setting up tables ready to bear food, chairs to receive hungry bodies.

Em wasn't there. Of course, I'd looked.

I propped myself up on my elbows, feeling the slope of the hill under my calves. I'd have to go down soon to help Old Ma Olga with the Harvest Spirit – as I'd done every year since they learned I had the gift of craft – but no one would miss me for a little while yet.

Towards the horizon, the jagged edges of the ancient city sparkled, its glassy ruins almost glowing in the dimming gold of the sun, as if someone had smashed the top off an egg and left behind the shell. Most of it had been overrun by vines, brush and wildflowers. Our Chronicles recounted how it had been built over a river, so when the city fell several hundred years ago, the forests around it reclaimed the remnants with speed, trapping relics under leaf, root and tendril.

Em used to joke that we could make a home there – on the inside.

"Think of it, Cee: so much ancient glass we could repurpose," she'd said, a curl of honey-brown hair at the base of her neck, her smile the pink fragrance of geranium, like every time she daydreamed. Tools I'd fashioned for her from the remains of an ancient flying machine jangled on the belt around her waist.

"Imagine how many photobioreactors we could build! We could make winters so much more comfortable – for all of us."

For some reason, she'd only bring this up whenever we were alone.

I'd let a moment of silence pass. Recent winters had seemed harsher, but I just couldn't see how our whole community would change our seasonal habits, traditions we'd kept year after year. We'd scavenged within the old city limits for materials now and again, but our tales told of something bad that had happened there a long time ago; changing minds would be no small feat.

"You honestly really think everyone would move?"

"Oh, Cee," Em had sighed, impatience creeping into her tone. "Once they realise it'll be consistently warmer, that we could cultivate a regular winter source of food – of course they will move."

We'd have to transform the place, make it liveable. Start small, show others how it could be done, until enough of us decide to work together. Not impossible, but every time I tried to imagine Em's vision of the future, my throat tightened. What if she overestimated my abilities? How rapidly would she tire of me?

Insecurity: the soft earth at the edge of a precipice.

It had been late spring then. I remembered because the poppies had just begun bursting out their vermillion petals, tiny red silk skirts fluttering in the breeze that still carried a chill. Em had stretched out beside me on this hill after breakfast, under this very elm tree. The remnants of the glass city caught the light differently in the mornings, a little less sparkle, a bit more haze. We'd sat here, stealing sips from a bottle of last winter's mead that we'd smuggled from Zed's father's reserves. My mind swept blank from the sheer bliss of being next to her, bare feet touching, legs lazily entwined, the meadow green against our skin – hers porcelain pale, mine tree-bark dark.

Desire: a turbulent propellant, not unlike the rocket fuel the ancients employed to such devastation.

"You could build what we'd need, I could adapt our algae culture, or perhaps, use some enzyme to the same effect." I couldn't tell if Em was simply thinking aloud, but her eyes had taken on a faraway daze. "It'd only take us a season or two to get it working. You'll see."

Em, the ever-optimist, the forever dreamer. Me? I just wasn't so good with change.

Uncertainty: a heavy fog at dawn's edge, the kind thick enough to blind you.

I wish I had known what I'd wanted, the way Em always seemed to. My fingers had twitched at that moment, aching to roll the twenty-sided die inside my pocket, but I'd known by then that Em didn't approve of my habit, so I fought against myself, battled against a cloud of guilt.

At some point, Em had shrugged, given in. "Anyway, seems you prefer to stick to the way things are."

That had stung a little, a puncture wound from a thorn under a rose. Then I'd tried to sound clever, forward-thinking. "But – what if we fail?"

"We could also succeed," Em promptly said. "You're always so either-or, Cee. We have the skills. Wouldn't you even want to try?"

Em had a gift with the abstract, with things we couldn't see with our eyes. She'd engineered the solar-powered lights for our settlement, built community ovens that required no fire to cook. Glass – I could work glass. I could work nearly every material I put my hands to: stone, clay, wood, metal, fibres from any plant. The glass could be restructured to become a vessel for the algae, but also insulation for us. We could grow some food through the cold season. Yes, we could've made it work, had we chosen to.

Had she chosen me.

Was that the last earnest conversation we'd had? I'd never quite known what she saw in me. She was an enigma, an endless source of beguiling mysteries.

Regret: a bottomless pit of stinking, rotting leaves, from which there was no way out.

Summer without Em had been eternal days and too-short nights. Every time I'd seen her since, she'd been with some others, younger or older. We still greeted each other, waved hello, but never spoke.

Grief: an open, bleeding wound that refused to heal.

Jealousy: All of the above.

Down the hill, it seemed as if all the lights had finally been set up. Not long before I would have to head down to find Olga-Ma.

From my left pocket, I extracted a small piece of paper that had gone soft from the number of times I'd handled it. It no longer rustled as I smoothed out its folds. A purple ticket – my name in Em's neat, handprinted capitals, the last one she'd given to me. It might even have been on that day when we were on this hill, when we last talked about the ancient glass city.

Purple tickets had evolved from an old practice; the Chronicles described a similar system which existed as far back as the time of the ancient city, explicit expressions for the wish of mutual intimacy. Arrangements with multiple people had been the norm then too.

They'd warned us not to be overtly attached to your first. I'd exchanged tickets with others throughout the summer, but – dare I admit it to myself – they were not Em. No one else was quite like Em. No one else made time irrelevant, days brim with possibilities and nights gentle with quiet ease.

Maybe she stopped asking for me because I'd thought all this time that she was joking – and she wasn't. Maybe it was my inertia, my indecisiveness. My either-or-ness. Maybe it was simply she found someone better who didn't fear her dreams.

A rustle came from my left, the sharp resinous scent of a rosemary bush being disturbed. A familiar figure, a slender silhouette sheathed in a loose work-wrap dress, pale legs long under the fluttering hem. My heart thumped.

Em. She'd walked up here barefoot.

Hastily, I tucked the purple ticket into my pocket.

Em sat down by my side, all honey-brown curls and geranium smile.

"Thought I'd find you here." Her silken voice – the sound of home I no longer had.

I pinched my hand. No, it wasn't a dream.

"Hello," I said, trying to appear casual, simultaneously chiding myself for it. I was happy to see her. Why couldn't I show it? "I'm just taking a break from the preparations."

That wasn't a lie, at least.

Her forehead furrowed ever so slightly, an expression I couldn't read. "Old Ma Olga sent me to look for you. Are you in trouble?"

Well, you found me, I wanted to say. Instead, I stared at my feet, two small creatures clad in worn leather shoes. "No, she just needs my help constructing the Spirit."

Silence: the weight of unspoken words crowding out the present.

My twenty-sided die still sat nestled between a clutch of clover and chamomile further along the ground. I itched to pick it up and roll it, but I didn't want Em to see – she hated the thing. So I leaned forward and pretended to brush something off my skirt, swiping my hand over the die at the same time, feeling its reassuringly sharp edges over the soft of the grass. I caught the number on top.

Seven. *Do something good for someone.*

Almost as if this thing contained an oracle.

Em was looking down the hill, and not at me.

"Where's Olga-Ma?" I asked, more to break the awkwardness of the moment than for the actual information.

She pointed to the tent of red-blue-green cloths that a few of us had erected some days ago, a temporary shelter standing where forest met field.

Beyond the woods, the glass city glittered. For a moment then, had the sun shone differently, had different wildflowers waved between the grass – we might have gone back in time to that day at the end of spring, when happier, possible futures spanned ahead of us.

Em stood first.

"Come on—" She extended a hand to me. Her fingers smooth, her grasp firm. How could I not recall their caress on my shoulder? Or the feel of them tracing my chin?

I retrieved the die from the grass as we got up. I wasn't quick enough to hide it.

"You still have that thing?" Em's eyebrows lifted, her green eyes examining mine. I shrivelled inside, words congealed in my throat. It didn't sound like an accusation, but still, guilt trapped me like the sticky middle of a spider's web.

She threw me a sideways glance but said no more. Perhaps one day I'd be able to show her, make her understand.

We sauntered down the hill, hand in hand, as if things had never changed. Perhaps they never did, and it had all just been in my own head?

"You've been busy?" It was a daft question, but curiosity scratched at my insides, a wildcat marking a tree.

"Kay will be getting committed in the spring, so there's just been endless arrangements."

Kay, her sister. "To whom?"

"To Vee, and also to Tey."

Everyone knew Vee, a nice enough guy, well-liked by most. Over a year ago, I had turned down their offer of a purple ticket. Tey, I knew less well.

"That's happy news!" I genuinely thought so. A commitment in the spring – something to look forward to.

Nearer to the tents, blackberry bushes sprawled down one side of the hill where they mingled with wild rosemary. Late season flowers dotted the meadow or exploded in bunches – vervain, burnet-saxifrage, harebells. I stooped down and picked a few, gathering them with my free hand, an idea brewing in my mind.

"Tell me," Em said, her voice a sudden shade of grey, her hand clasping mine tighter.

"Yes?"

"Cee – are you happy?"

That took me by surprise. The wildflowers in my unsteady hand shook their little floral heads. "Em, I—"

I didn't know what to say.

A little sigh escaped those lips. Em looked away. "You never asked for me anymore, I assumed you found happiness elsewhere."

What?

"Em—" I swallowed. How could I put this into words? "I thought… I thought that maybe I was holding you back…"

You, your dreams – your dreams like murmurings of starlings.

She gripped my hand, dragging me to an awkward stop. Her gaze pierced mine, a flash of an undecipherable fire behind those green eyes. I would gladly melt in that fire.

"Really, Cee, you're so silly sometimes."

We'd reached the edge of the settlement, and suddenly people were everywhere, busying themselves with various tasks ahead of the festival. More to say, but now wasn't the time.

Em nodded towards the tent where Olga was waiting. She gave my hand a final squeeze, and mouthed *later* – a promise that made my skin sing. Letting go of her hand was like losing an anchor. She vanished into the bustle of other bodies, the noise of the settlement suddenly unbearable after the calm of the hill.

I wanted badly to follow her and say, *yes, yes, let's go – to the ancient glass city. Let's make it work. Tomorrow, we could go tomorrow.*

Instead, I slid around the settlement towards the field and paused at the door flap of Olga-Ma's tent, watching her shadow move about inside.

I'd read in our Chronicles that when communities decided to split and settle separately, they would take a piece of the Spirit – the symbolic winter home of the Harvest Goddess – after the Festival of the Full Corn Moon and bring it with them to the new place as a blessing.

I could detach a section from this year's Spirit after the festival. I could take it to Em – a token to show her I was ready to go with her.

But if I couldn't tell anyone, would that count as stealing?

*

If Old Ma Olga had been impatient, she didn't show it.

"There you are, Cee-cee," her warm, sonorous voice called from inside the tent when I lifted open the door flap.

She'd already sharpened her sickle. Together we walked up to the last sheaf of wheat, rye and vetch standing in the field, a patch of browning grasses at the edge of the food forest we cultivated whenever we settled here. Some of these trees and plants had probably been here as long as the ancient glass city. The ones we liked to eat, we helped to reseed, resow. For the others, we let nature do its thing.

On our way back to the tent, I held Old Ma Olga's sickle for her.

"A tall one this year, I think," she said, her arms full of the symbolic harvest. "To signify how the early rains helped the plants flourish so early, that we had such a bountiful harvest this year."

I nodded and got to work, the die in my skirt pocket shifting as I moved around Olga-Ma's worktable. Grabbing a handful of wheat, I wove a foundation for the Spirit's winter home.

Eighteen. *Focus on the task at hand.*

I'd only really understood our annual ritual with the Harvest Spirit after I'd had the luck of the draw. Every year, all the children in the settlement were invited to draw from a pile of straw; whoever extracted the longest got to lead the procession, carrying the Harvest Spirit from the field to the festival. Six years ago, I had been the one blessed with good fortune. The idea wasn't to craft the likeness of the Harvest Goddess herself – more to fashion a home for her essence to overwinter in. During my turn that year, Old Ma Olga realised I had the gift of craft and material. She used to make the Spirit with her own hands, but the more persistent the pain in her fingers became, the more she relied on me.

After the festival, the Spirit would journey with us to our winter settlement and pass the cold seasons in Old Ma Olga's caravan until the following spring. Then we'd bury it back into the ground so it could work its magic for the new year.

I had no idea if that would be possible in the ancient city. If the whole place had been paved over beneath the wild green, like what I'd read in the Chronicles, how could Em and I even grow anything?

The fear-laced anxiety came again like a tidal wave. My hands shook. A stalk of wheat slipped from my fingers. I very nearly reached for the die, but remembered myself. Olga-Ma might be busy with something else behind me, but the rattling of the die on the worktable would catch her attention, and I'd have to make uncomfortable excuses. How might I ever reconcile Em's dislike of the die? How could I ever explain – just reciting its list of actions calmed me down?

"What's eating away at you, my Cee, hmm?" Old Ma Olga's voice jolted me out of my thoughts.

Without paying conscious attention, I'd somehow completed the foundations for the Spirit, and already begun the second, decorative layer. Olga-Ma had been working through the knots on a string and winding it up into a tidy ball.

"Nothing." I kept my face expressionless. How did she know?

"You've always been a quiet one, but usually..." She paused. "Well, I don't know, I'll let you tell me."

When I still said nothing, Olga-Ma spoke, her voice soft. "Cee, look at me."

I dropped the bundle I'd been working with, did as I was told.

"My little rabbit, you looked positively gripped with fear right then. What are you afraid of?"

Fear: a cavernous ravine, a night creature waiting in the shadows to devour you, a future with endless possibilities.

What was I afraid of? Everything.

I exhaled, it came out as a sigh. Somehow, Olga-Ma heard the voices in my head without me saying a single word.

Suddenly, she dropped the ball of string she'd been fiddling with and wrapped her arms around me. My body stiffened at her touch. The ball unwound itself, rolling haphazardly across the uneven floor.

"Oh little one, you never did get much time with your Ma, did you?"

The community had been good to me since the day Ma didn't come back from a hunt, barely a year after Pa fell ill and didn't wake up one day. I was always fed, clothed, given a place to sleep. I had free rein over our Chronicles and the settlement, but, always, something seemed incomplete.

That time I brought the Harvest Spirit from the field to the festival, I'd looked back into the crowd, knowing that Ma and Pa would be so proud of me. I'd searched for them in the sea of faces – only to remember they'd never see me do that walk of a lifetime. They would never see me raise the Spirit up high, how I held my poise, my feet leading the procession in a steady rhythm.

They'd never see me do anything, ever again.

Grief: a slippery, slimy slug eating its way through a fragile leaf, the tattered residue of one's soul.

I shook my head, fighting the tears building up behind my eyes. I didn't want to cry right now. The die felt hard under my thumb in my pocket.

Three. *Acknowledge your anguish.*

A shuffle at the tent flap made Old Ma Olga release me from her embrace.

"Do you want me yet, Olga-Ma?" A small, but confident voice piped up from the entrance.

Jay, barely a teen, this year's lucky child to carry the Harvest Spirit to the centre of the festival. Already tall for their age, Jay's whole being buzzed with anticipation. I'd been that chosen child once. That excitement: a bellyful of fluttering butterflies. Did I also wear such joy on my face?

I quickly wiped my cheeks. But Jay spotted the Harvest Spirit and skipped right over for a closer look.

"Olga-Ma! Cee! This is *beautiful!*"

I had to smile; I might have outdone myself by weaving in the end-of-season wildflowers. Unlike the usual beige figure, this year's Spirit stood laced with colour: white, orange, pale purple and a gentle pink.

Neither Olga-Ma nor Jay would have been able to see, but I'd built it so a small bundle of the harvest under the decorative layer would release with a tug of twine.

"It's nearly finished," I declared. "See that pole down here?" I showed Jay where their hands would go. "I've carved little notches for your fingers, should make it easier to carry."

I'd not forgotten the slippery pole I'd had to handle that day when I was the chosen child.

A cacophony of voices crescendoed outside the tent. The other children joining the procession were ready. The moment Olga-Ma left to speak to them, I slipped a cleaning cloth off her worktable and stuffed it into my pocket.

Then, I gave the working twine one last twist around the body of the Harvest Spirit. For some reason I blew on it as I would a candle. Perhaps to infuse it with my own, unspoken wishes.

*

The sun hadn't yet entirely dipped below the horizon by the time I joined the end of the procession, but already, the wind had turned cold. Winter might come early.

I kept myself well behind everyone else. I wasn't part of the troupe, but I wanted to be close enough to keep an eye on the Spirit should anything happen.

Jay held it up high, using their height to advantage. Olga-Ma followed several steps behind, surrounded by the youngest children. Giggles, laughter. The walk from the field to the feast wasn't that long, but I could still remember the weight of the Spirit I'd had to balance above my head, how that short walk felt like an eternity.

We could smell the food even before we reached the tents. The punch of herbs and spices, the meatiness of stews prepared from yesterday's hunts, the vegetable roasts. Cheers erupted as we got close to the open clearing where the tables had been set, the adults parting a way for us to walk through. One of the musicians – the drummer – had started up a rhythm, the steady pace of an enthusiastic march.

We headed towards the main table at the far end of the clearing where it faced the bonfire, already lit and blazing. With deliberate care, Jay set the Spirit down and Old Ma Olga slipped it onto a stand someone else had prepared, a large weighted spool with a hole in it. The hole was a little too big for the pole, but the Spirit stood up fine. I made a mental note to build something better next year.

A tiny swell of pride warmed my chest; this year's Spirit had something special about it. How hard would it be to replicate another? This might have been the first year I didn't agonise too much, let the textures of the sheaves guide me as to where they might go, lost myself in the joy of making something with my hands.

I felt for the die in my pocket.

Sixteen. *Dance at every opportunity.*

All at once, other musicians joined the lone drummer, and they burst into a lively little jig. A few carried the textured tune on stringed instruments, someone kept time on a tambourine. People began to sway and twirl. Someone hoisted a wild hog over the fire. Freshly-baked breads, generous bowls of root salad, large plates of rice and beans made their rounds on the feasting tables.

Did I want to dance? I didn't get a chance to think before Jay dragged me into the heaving crowd.

For a brief moment I caught sight of Em, fixing a string of lights that had stopped working. A song or two afterwards, she sat at the edge of a table, deep in conversation with a young man older than both of us, his blond hair pulled back into a ponytail – perhaps Zed's brother. She seemed to be having a good time. Old jealousy soared, a wily shark breaking through the surface, but I swallowed it. No, I should be glad she was having a good time, even without me.

A herby aroma permeated the air when the first soup was served, a number of dancers peeled off to eat. I took the chance, beelining for the table where Em had been.

She was no longer there.

Disappointment: the damp bottom of a well.

What had she meant by "later"?

The sun had given way to the rising full moon, rendering the night bruised and darkened. We pushed the tables back towards the edges when more people joined the dance.

I slipped away from the crowd and walked towards the Harvest Spirit, approaching the figure from behind. The bonfire and solar lights lit up the dance, but out here beyond the feasting tables, shadows lurked.

My heartbeat loud in my ears, I reached towards the fold where I'd hidden the end of a second piece of twine.

"Beautiful work this year, Cee," a voice said.

I thrusted my hand back into my pocket. The die hit hard against my knuckles. It was only Tey – one of the young men Kay would be committing to. "I don't know how you do it."

"Thank you," I managed to say, my breath ragged. "Just practice, I guess."

"Anyhow, thought you should hear that." Tey flashed me a smile, and disappeared back into the group of dancers.

I reached again, shoving my hand into the right side of the Spirit, just under a sheaf that fanned outwards. My fingers found the hidden twine – I tugged, hard. A small, neat bundle of wheat and rye came away silently, straight into my palm. I breathed out through my teeth, a low whistle of relief. Using the cloth I'd taken from Olga-Ma's worktable, I wrapped the bundle and slipped it deep into my pocket.

Probably best to drop it back at my tent, then rejoin the dance. No one need ever know. Tomorrow, I would find Em, and we could start forming plans, make our way to the ancient city.

The tent I slept in stood furthest away from the centre. A plain, dark green affair, I'd made a few custom adjustments so I could keep the external door flap open on hot summer nights without anyone seeing inside. In winter, it stayed warm. I liked my quiet and everyone knew it, so they always let me settle a little further from everyone else. Behind me, the music throbbed, the fire burned, the dancers spun.

Someone seized my arm, I stifled a scream.

Em's face emerged from the shadows, framed by those honey-brown curls, carrying that geranium smile.

"Sorry, didn't meant to startle you."

I choked down my panic.

"Why are—"

"Been waiting for you, that's all."

She drew me into an urgent embrace, her lips soft, tasting of mead. Then she reached for my hand, placing something that rustled into my palm. I knew what it was without having to look – a purple ticket. My heart pounded, my mouth dry. When she pulled back to speak, her breath was shallow.

"I knew you'd try to escape early." She gestured towards the pulse of the festivities. Laughed. "You're so predictable, Cee."

Desire: a fire pooling deep that hungered for more to burn.

I might have been predictable, but there was more to me than that.

"I want to… to show you something first." I reached into my pocket, feeling for the cloth bundle.

A loud scream pierced the darkness. The music stopped. A loud crash. More shouts. Different voices yelled.

Wild-eyed, Em and I exchanged a glance. She moved first, back towards the dance. I ran after her flying hair.

By the time we wove through the tents back to the feasting, the crowd had gone largely silent. A sniffle here, a sob there. The smell gave it away first, a smokiness, a greenness, something being freshly burned.

In the middle over the fire, a burning pile of the Harvest Spirit, engulfed in flames.

Em grasped my shoulder. "Cee…"

I couldn't speak.

Someone must have bumped against it, knocked it off its precarious stand – straight into the bonfire.

Old Ma Olga was nowhere to be seen. She might have already retired for the night.

The die in my pocket weighed heavy, but I didn't need it, not this time. Somehow, the solution was crystal clear. The Chronicles had always been explicit: what we fashioned year after year was only a temporary home, not the Spirit itself. This needn't be the disaster everyone feared.

"I can make another," I said out loud, surprising myself. The conversational noise around me dropped as people realised I'd spoken.

"I can make another," I repeated, louder this time.

All of them – the dancers, the musicians, the feasting crowd – stood and stared at me, confused. In the smoky dimness, I tried to meet their gaze, one by one.

"The Spirit is here, yes, it is in what we grow, but it's also in all of us." I threw an arm in a wide circle. "Here's what we need to do: each of you – go back to your home, bring me a piece of your harvest, however small. I'll remake the Spirit's winter home. Right here, now."

At first, no one moved. Then one of them shuffled towards a tent, another followed suit. One by one, they hurried away.

Em, Jay and Tey cleared the feasting table so I could use it as a workspace. Material started flowing in: ears of corn, bundles of grapes, apples, a small sheaf of wheat, some rye.

I got to work, arranging and binding this to that, focussing on the natural shapes of the bounty and gave way to how they wanted to show themselves.

The small bundle from the old Spirit felt heavy in my pocket. The thought struck so suddenly, that looking back now, it was as if a higher force slipped the idea into my head. I took the bundle out and split it in two. I'd keep half for the city, but doing this meant part of the old Spirit could live in the new.

Someone started a song. One of the musicians picked up a fiddle, and once again people began to dance, if slower, less frenzied.

At some point, Em had her hand on my shoulder, at some point she moved away.

Time melted, the world folded backwards as my fingers worked to construct a new Harvest Spirit – affording me a kind of peace.

"Here," said Em. In her hands were wildflowers from the hill, our hill.

I smiled, and braided them in.

And suddenly, the second Harvest Spirit I'd made in a day was finished.

Tey helped me balance the new Spirit on a more stable, stump of wood.

Cheers drowned out the music for a long moment, then the dance resumed.

A different thought entered my head: next harvest moon, I should teach someone else to do what I do, so none of these traditions would be forgotten.

*

The air cooled my back, my legs felt stiff with each step up the hill. The moon had begun its descent, a silver disc losing its shine, but still round, still full. From the settlement below, sounds of dance and song floated on the night breeze, muted by the shush of grass and the whispering leaves of trees.

Em fell in step beside me. I took her arm, like old times.

"I wanted to tell you I'd missed you," she said. "All summer."

"Was that why you were hovering near my tent tonight?"

She let out a soft, embarrassed giggle. "I suppose I owe you an apology, of sorts."

"You do?" My feet stopped, so did hers.

Em spun me around to face her, her serious gaze half lit by the glow of the moon.

"I never asked you what you wanted. I might have said you were predictable. But truth is, I can't read you, Cee."

"I'm not a book."

She laughed, and clasped me close.

We made our way to the elm tree, the grass damp under our skirts, yarrow feathering under my fingers, clovers cloistering under the fading night.

I pointed at the horizon, at the glass city in the distance.

"I came here often, so I could look at that over there, like we used to do. Dream about what we might have done if we'd gone." I caught myself. "Think about it, I mean. You did all the dreaming."

She chuckled, the breeze teasing her honey-brown hair.

I took a deep breath. "Do you want to go tomorrow?"

Her eyes widened, her mouth dropped open. "Did you just say what I thought you said?"

For an answer, I pulled out the bundle wrapped in its cloth from my pocket. Smaller than what I originally intended, but it still hefted a decent sized bulk.

"A part of the Spirit will come with us, we can start something new. And when the next harvest comes around, we could return and meet everyone else at an appointed place. Will you come with me?"

Given how hard Em hugged me then, I was worried I'd lose the bundle altogether. The moon hid behind a cloud, I could no longer see her face, but I was sure that she was wearing her geranium smile when she planted a crimson kiss on my cheek.

The die in my pocket shifted as we laid down on the grass.

Nine. *Give way to courage, seize the day.*

Or perhaps, seize the moon.

When Em wasn't looking, I tossed the die under the elm tree.

Fear: something one should never face alone.

Hope: the dawn of a new day, because no sunrise is the same as any other.

Swimming-Hunger – A Rusted Drum – A Ruinous Discovery

Rayn Epremian

First Report – 21 Days Before Launch

My moniker is HR-33 of the Human Resources and Operations Department and I attest to the honesty, accuracy, and completeness of the notes that follow.

I have been assigned observation duties of the Engineer, E-48, to ensure his wellbeing and sound mind as we near the critical stages of the launch of the Recruitment project. It is an honour to be entrusted with this role, as human observation is an almost antiquated practice now that we have such effective surveillance equipment across the OneCorp Campus here on Mars. I will take on this responsibility with utmost humility, gravity, and rigour as required for the Board's review. I will leave nothing out. The Board will decide in its authority and wisdom which parts are relevant, as only a doctor can diagnose if a disease is present. My role is less than nurse: simply to record what may or may not be symptoms. I will observe only, and shall not meddle or intervene unless the Board explicitly bids me do so.

This morning I entered the Facility at 08:20, ten minutes prior to the official start to the Workday, as is customary, and shared the elevator with the Engineer; he is quite punctual. The Engineer seems to already recognise me on sight, but I have no reason to believe he suspects I am observing him in any greater capacity than we all routinely observe one another on Campus. He greeted me with the courtesy expected of my rank; his demeanour was appropriately subservient, not ingratiating. He has not asked what my role is in the department, but no one does; my presence is accepted in all Facilities on account of my HR badge. To question it would be a breach of custom, if not Policy.

I monitored E-48's activity throughout the Workday. From his computer screen, I could see he worked on the code for the rocket's trajectory to Earth. It will arrive there thirteen days after its launch, in the middle of one of the primitive winter 'spiritual' festivals many of the Old Colonies on Earth still observe. Disrupting this festival will assist the dissemination of the Recruitment messages carried within. The Engineer's work appeared meticulous in regard to this timeline and all other matters within my understanding. He left the Facility at 18:15, after the rest of his subordinates; most appropriate. I did not descend the elevator with him so as not to arouse suspicion, but departed five minutes afterwards and followed him to his sector.

In the evening I watched his apartment from across the street, from a vacant apartment behind a window used as a permanent Ad screen, so that he could not see me. It felt strange to be so hidden, illicit as hiding is to us on Campus, where all things are in the open in keeping with the OneCorp tenet of Transparency; but I accepted it as it is necessary to the greater cause of the targetted surveillance I am carrying out.

The emptiness of the apartment itself was also strange; so different from my comfortable, curated home full of Company items I have earned over my years of Employment. Sounds echoed; there was even a draught unusual to the Martian climate. The Ads are important, to remind us to fill such spaces, to keep earning and spending.

However, I did lose sight of the Engineer's dwelling during the Evening Ad Reel, when all windows are converted to screens on both sides for this important purpose. To account for this blind spot in future, I have requested use of traditional audio-recording devices, as antiquated as they are, to be placed within his apartment.

On this occasion I observed nothing out of the ordinary. He ate his rations at the appropriate time, bathed, and did not leave his bed after the 22:00 curfew when the lights in the East Sector go out.

My initial estimate at this juncture is that there is nothing out of the ordinary about the Engineer, and he is a sound-minded Employee fit to complete his duties. However, I will continue to monitor him, as I've been charged to do, and as the extreme import of his case requires, and leave judgement up to the Board.

Second Report – 20 Days Before Launch

This morning, to disguise the fact that I had stayed overnight in his sector, I departed early, right after the Morning Ad Reel, and took the train back towards my own apartment before going to the Facility. At the West Sector Train Station, I saw something disturbing. Beneath the official signage, '*OneCorp. One Body,*' someone had painted, in a horrible, dripping red scrawl, '*One Corpse.*' I submitted a notice for clean-up immediately. I count it fortunate that due to the early hour, few Employees would have seen it before it was removed. I humbly suggest to the Board that an increased number of video cameras may be useful on the Campus train lines, to catch the perpetrators, who in addition to this brass act, must have been outdoors after curfew. Where they contrived to obtain the paint from is another question for the Company Policy Administration Department. It is an unacceptable, offensive debasement of the OneCorp brand. I apologise for the inclusion here, as this observation does not relate directly to the Engineer; however, I feel I would be remiss to leave it out as any dutiful Employee, and especially as a member of the Operations Department. I admit my blood boiled at the sight of this slight against the company – but I shall dwell on it no further here.

Thanks to the impeccable engineering of OneCorp, I arrived at the Facility without further incident. My diversion allowed me to arrive from a different direction to the Engineer just in time to share the elevator with him. He greeted me as courteously as the day before.

There was one other in the elevator with us, a woman. I have not seen her at the Facility before, but she had the correct identification badge to access the elevator. She too issued the appropriate greetings. I observed that she and the Engineer held eye contact for a protracted period of time, but I was perhaps looking for something to find remarkable, as it is my role to observe. I leave all interpretation, as ever, up to the Board.

I once again made myself as unobtrusive as possible throughout the day, whilst keeping a watchful eye on the Engineer. He worked at his station all day as usual. On two occasions I saw him staring blankly, or so it seemed to me, in some manner of distraction. He may indeed have been puzzling out some technical problem outside of my domain of knowledge. However, I saw him visibly start out of these thoughts, as though into wakefulness. I looked up the phenomenon on my dicto-pad later and found the archaic term 'reverie' seemed to describe this accurately. I must admit it alarmed me somewhat to find such an old, duly buried word fit this occurrence I had seen only hours before. The idea that dreams, the dangers of which are avoided as much as possible during sleep thanks to our advanced sleep-cycle technology preventing that precarious mode known as REM, might be experienced during waking hours – and *Working* hours! – is indeed disturbing.

The rest of the day progressed as usual. The Engineer consumed his rations, and observed the Evening Ad Reel attentively (thanks to the newly installed audio surveillance devices, I could hear him reciting along with them and responding as expected). As it was a Fourthday, his assigned partner for this quarter visited his apartment. I listened to their congress and heard nothing abnormal. She departed at 21:15, and the Engineer washed and was in his bed alone at 22:00.

Third Report – 18 Days Before Launch

The woman C-21 – I have identified her from the elevator encounter as Communications personnel – has been to see the Engineer. I checked the Randomised Sexual Rotation Register, and she is not his assigned partner for this quarter – I would have recognized her from the Fourthday visit, and of course Employees who work the same shifts in the same Facilities are never paired, as it can cause distraction during the Workday. This is of course one of the reasons I was selected for this task; the Board has seen, in its infinite wisdom, my flaws and made of them advantages. My own lack of normal sexual desire, while an obvious shortcoming, makes me less susceptible to the likeliest distractions and temptations of this observational role. We have seen, too many times before, Employees converted to delinquency through the means of seduction, one of the numerous reasons for the longstanding obligatory, token-monitored Sexual Rotation System, with randomised pairings sanctioned and assigned by OneCorp. Thus, this unauthorized visit upon the Engineer by C-21 is most alarming. I worry she has identified his important role in the Recruitment and could be trying to seduce him to some cause using these illicit meetings – what that cause might be remains to be seen.

Please advise if I should intervene.

Fourth Report – 16 Days Before Launch

The Engineer left the Facility on his thirty-minute ration break today for the first time since I have begun my observations. I followed at a distance, as though I, too, were on a casual breaktime stroll for my physical health. Luckily, he went to the Campus Park, a public place where many Employees take their exercise on the concentric asphalt paths, so I blended in easily. I am confident he did not see me – and if he did, there would be nothing strange to make of it.

I suspected, feared, that perhaps he was going to another illicit meeting with C-21. However, it soon became evident that E-48 was visiting a colleague of his, R-9, of the Decorative Engineering Department (formerly the Art-Works Dept.), who is designing the new pyramid sculpture for the Campus Park. I sat on a bench some way away and listened to their conversation, which I have transcribed below:

E-48: R-9! Have you been productive?

R-9: Friend, it's been too long. You've been a busy bee up in the Facility for weeks.

E: R, you always use phrases I don't understand. What is a 'bee'?

R: Some kind of bug. No, not a computer virus – an insect. They went extinct back on Earth a long time ago.

E: That hardly seems appropriate.

R: They were engineers, like you.

E: Like us.

R: Sure.

E: We're not extinct, though.

R: Not yet, my friend!

E: Well, how is your new Art-Work coming along?

R: Fine. It's not hard. Just shapes. It's going to be a pyramid. Right here in the middle of the Park. In the middle of the whole Campus Dome, really.

E: It sounds perfect. And quite an honour, no? But I don't know what you mean, just shapes. What else would it be?

R: You're right. Nothing else would be… *appropriate*. Anyway, pyramids, you know, some people used to believe—

E: R!

(At this point, R-9 laughed quietly in his throat.)

E: Don't laugh, you can't go saying things like that.

R: All right, all right. Tell me about your project, then. How is the rocket?

(R-9 was chewing on the end of his stylus, a disgusting habit.)

E: It's going to plan. We're on track for the launch date. I just have a few equations to work out, which are giving me trouble. And I've been… I don't know, distracted, these last few days.

(Needless to say, this caught my attention, which was already focussed upon them!)

R: That doesn't sound like you. Not daydreaming on the job, are you?

E: Daydreaming! No! No… well. It's troubling, R. Maybe you would call it that. Old-fashioned, foolish word! And yet… I do think about her, when she isn't there.

R: Her! The plot thickens.

E: What plot?

R: I mean the story is getting interesting.

E: There's no story! There are no stories. R-9, are you all right?

R: Fine, E. Fine.

E: Well, it's time to go back. It was good to see you.

E-48 left R-9 then, and despite his words, his face looked troubled – as, no doubt, was mine. The Decorative Engineer R-9 is clearly a worrying person. These old words he uses, the *ideas* he seems to have – we all know 'artists' are dangerous individuals and cannot be allowed in OneCorp. I, like E-48, personally cannot imagine what he was talking about with regard to something other than 'just shapes' but it obviously cannot be tolerated. All Employees know that there can be no Art-Works depicting people, 'scenes' or, pardon my use of R-9's term, '*stories*'. The only viable, valid Art-Work is geometry. Anything else is outmoded Earth nonsense, like their seasonal festivals and 'elections'. If R-9 is not already on a list for Review, I humbly recommend his name be taken under consideration.

Apologies for the digression – I will return now to the individual at hand, E-48. I daresay his replies to R-9 show the thinking of a reliable Employee: he does not seem to have been corrupted, and reports that his work is on track. However, the worrying matter of 'daydreaming' seems to confirm my concern, and if this is slowing his progress in any way this is unacceptable. It is clear the woman C-21 is responsible – could she be trying to disrupt the launch, or is this an unfortunate but ignorant consequence of an illicit attraction? Either way, she has broken Company Policy. I leave any action on the matter in the hands of the capable Board.

One last observation to note – I had the displeasure of seeing that graffiti again as I left the Park. On a metal bench, in the same red paint as before – '*One Corpse*'.

Fifth Report – 12 Days Before Launch

C-21 has visited E-48 twice more this week – on neither occasion were tokens logged. E-48 has not visited C-21; she always comes to his apartment. He never seems to expect her, yet he always lets her in. They didn't speak much on the first two occasions. On the third, tonight, they had the following conversation:

E-48: I'm worried about R-9.

C-21: The Art-Worker?

E: He's an Engineer, like me.

C: No one's like you.

E: Don't say that. I'm like everyone. But R isn't. That's why I'm worried about him. He says such strange things. Old words. Like you.

C: And me? Are you worried about me?

E: All the time. You shouldn't be here—

C: I am here now. So let's talk about this another time.

E: But if you aren't here, how will we talk about—

At this point, she interrupted him by kissing him, and they engaged in further sexual activity.

E-48 seems to be holding out against these corrupting individuals, but I really recommend intervention so that the task will not be so hard. So far, he remains a reliable Employee, but his mind and the project are at risk, a risk that could be removed. Why he chooses to interact with these dangerous people remains a mystery.

His assigned partner for this quarter has not visited him this week.

Sixth Report – 10 Days Before Launch

Today they, E-48 and C-21, went together to the Museum of Earth, where the archaic practices of pre-corporatisation are kept for educational purposes; with clear knowledge of the undeveloped past, we can arm ourselves against similar follies in the future. This was the first time I have observed the two of them together outside of the Engineer's apartment, or their brief interactions in the Facility. I have not intervened, and shall continue to await further instruction.

Today, something odd happened. Where usually during their

illicit meetings they engage in sexual activity, today they did not. At first, I thought perhaps their attraction had run its course, and we were now in the clear, as surely they would then stop seeing each other and the Engineer would be safe from temptation. But in fact something stranger, and more concerning, may be taking place; their physical habit has given way to something else. Today, they simply walked together through the various exhibits, at times speaking – of nothing of import as far as I could tell, unless they have designed a strange and elaborate code. No discernible ideas or plans. Simply… 'small talk'. Yet it did not seem small.

It is difficult to explain on the page; I have tried transcribing the conversation, but it looks like nothing when written down. It was not the words themselves that seemed noteworthy, but their behaviour – or perhaps the very act of their speaking. Even their not-speaking. Perhaps more so.

Apologies, I am not being clear; it is difficult, I am not at all sure what it is I am trying to describe. They smiled, and once or twice touched hands. Watching them, a strange feeling came over me, a sort of shyness, as though I should not have been watching. I have never experienced this in the past, even during their sexual congresses. Another feeling, stranger still, then grew within me. A sort of opening, or emptiness, like the hunger one feels after a long and healthful swim in the Recreation Centre. But there is no Cafeteria at hand to quench this hunger with a protein ration. I don't know what it is. It is as though there is more space inside me than I knew. I suddenly found myself hollow, like the steel oil drums in the Campus Storage Centre.

Alarmed, I stopped at the Physio on the way home. The doctors say all is well. Of course, I could not speak to them of the day's events without sharing classified information about my assignment, so I gave no details. I can only assume this is part of some tactic to throw my focus off the scent of C-21's perfidy. I still have no reason to believe she or the Engineer suspects me of being the one on their trail. But surely she is attempting to gather him to some nefarious purpose. I shall catch them in the act soon enough.

Seventh Report – 9 Days Before Launch

Today I experienced the swimming-hunger again. In truth, it has grown worse. It is almost a physical sickness, though I know I am perfectly healthy. I felt it first in my throat, and worried I was taking ill with Spring influenza, but the doctors have once again assured me I am perfectly healthy. I must stop taking their time on these imaginary matters. But I digress.

It was at the Engineer's apartment. I was, of course, across the street, in the empty apartment, listening through the audio-recording devices. C-21 went over, and I expected to hear the usual sounds of sex, or some incriminating speech I could record to resolve this matter. But what I heard instead was simply laughter. Mingled laughter, his and hers. And strangely, when I heard that sound, the swimming-hunger came upon me once more, and seemed to grow in me like a mould, carving out more space. I became, all of a sudden, a rusted drum.

I despise these conspirators, for they have shown me what must be called *loneliness*, where before I knew no such thing. A discovery, a ruinous discovery. In witnessing the fragility of their companionship, I have been cast from the paradise of robust, unwavering community. I suddenly feel – and it makes me ill, physically ill, to feel it, so traitorous is the thought – that I would give anything, do anything, for a moment of mingled laughter. For something so fleeting and fragile! I know of course that this is utter foolishness. It is the traitors who have condemned themselves to exile. I am safe in the masses of *us*. In OneCorp there can be no such thing as loneliness. Yet a perverse part of my mind desires it. It craves that peculiar emptiness, and more, its poisonous corollary temptation – that there might be a way to fill it.

Oh how exquisite, to be yet unfinished. To have such space within. It is almost, no it is indeed, a pain to me. But it is a pain like an itch, which, once scratched, feels almost worthwhile. The promise of relief, of a mysterious balm, is somehow greater than the emptiness. The discomfort becomes anticipation. Like hunger when one is approaching the Cafeteria, making the rations all the more flavourful, all the more filling. Is this what normal individuals feel in regard to sexual attraction? But this is something else. I do not know what sustenance it is I crave, what satisfies this gap I've found in me. But the nature of the gap is like that question – it is the very *wanting* to know the answer. A dangerous curiosity, to be sure.

I include this here in the interests of full transparency, as is the solemn promise of OneCorp, and so that these effects may be observed in case this is a psychological attack of some kind by the truants; so that we may investigate the cause, and prevent this curiosity, perhaps disseminate the answers clearly to Employees that find themselves questing along these precarious lines, or provide some other solution. I find myself reflecting on the Company Policy advice to transgressing Employees: *pain will set you free.*

Eighth Report – 7 Days Before Launch

E-48 and C-21 returned to the Museum today. It was most suspicious, I thought, to visit twice in one week. After all, the average Employee only visits once a year as a reminder of the failures of pre-corporatised humanity. To my inexpressible distress, I was right.

I followed them through the exhibits, keeping distance, as it is never very busy inside the Museum and so my trailing them might have been noticed. I do not think it was. But it wouldn't have mattered. I followed them to the back of the Exhibit of the Nuclear Family, where they left the building through a maintenance exit. I followed them through, out to the back of the building, which is near the Southern edge of Campus. But that is where I stopped, for I could not follow where they went – they vanished!

Beyond the translucent wall of the Campus Dome, outside the terraformed, oxygen-rich environment where we are able to live, thrive, Work. There is no breathable air outside. I did not follow, I could not; they would not have lasted more than a minute out in the Beyond. I take full responsibility for their deaths. There must have been some sign I missed, some indication that they were planning Resignation. Recruitment is no doubt now at risk, the schedule disrupted, perhaps even impossible, with the Resignation of the Engineer. And on my watch! I am ashamed. I am almost tempted to Resign as well – but I will wait for my Termination if that is the judgement of the Board.

Or so I thought. I wrote the first part of this report, but before I submitted it – I admit I was hesitating, out of shame – the unthinkable occurred. I saw the Engineer! E-48. From my viewpoint in the empty apartment across the street, where I was cleaning up to depart, I saw him return home. He was unscathed, if a little dazed – but then, so was I, at the sight of him, who should have been a ghost. Fanciful notion, I know, but I was shocked into fancy, thinking myself delirious. But no, it was perfectly real. The Engineer E-48 is alive.

So is C-21. I saw her go to his apartment sometime later, and their conversation, the recordings of which I have attached – note that horrid phrase, 'One Corpse', repeated thrice – proved what I had suspected: that she led him outside. According to C-21, there is some kind of group hiding out there, beyond the Dome. I don't understand this, and find it difficult to believe, but perhaps this group has found a way to create a separate, smaller dome attached to the Campus, like the parasite they are. In any case, her intentions are clear: to tempt the Engineer away, to that other place, before the Recruitment strategy is completed, and to disrupt the launch for their own purposes. If this isn't against Company Policy, truly, what can be?

Ninth Report – 6 Days Before Launch

As the Board is aware, following its directive, the Company Policy Administrators collected C-21 today. Her Contract has been Terminated. She will no longer be a risk to the completion of the Recruitment strategy.

I did not attend the Termination, as I was still performing my surveillance of the Engineer, and he did not attend. This omission on his part might be considered suspicious, rebellious even, but then again, he was at work in the Facility on the rocket, so perhaps he has simply rediscovered his priorities, as intended.

Tenth Report – 5 Days Before Launch

I am continuing to monitor the Engineer, to make sure he is not distracted by grief following the Termination of C-21.

He seems more focussed than ever. In fact, he is coming in earlier, leaving the Facility later, than he ever did before. He only takes five or ten of his allotted thirty minutes at the midday mealtime to replenish himself. He has not gone on any walks to the Park, has had no further meetings with R-9 or any other individuals. The launch of the rocket is on track, Recruitment will not be delayed. If this is the Engineer's grief, then pain, indeed, has set him free.

And yet. Mine seems to trap me. I thought I would feel lighter in the absence of C-21 – unburdened, newly healthy, finally able to shake off the strange disease the two had laid upon me. Yet it persists. It grows stronger, a parasite hollowing out more and more of my insides. I thought destroying their connection would remove the idea of it from my mind forever, wipe it clean, restore me, but I feel the loss of their companionship almost as though it were my own. Instead, now I am still empty, but feel no hope of filling the emptiness; there is no blueprint for such an outcome. Surely this is better, the hope must be the most painful part of all – surely it will fade in time, replaced once more by the comfortable, complacent unanimity, the familiar oneness, of the Company. Surely…

Eleventh Report – 4 Days Before Launch

I've discovered a distressing action on the part of the Engineer. He has tampered with the Recruitment Pack. Where it is, of course, meant to be an accurate and affirmative depiction of OneCorp to invite unevolved humans of Earth to join our Workforce, to find purpose in labour, to be part of us, the Engineer has written libelous accusations, alluding to violence and coercion. Coercion!

He even wrote that the land outside the Campus was perfectly habitable, a dangerous lie to be sure – though it would explain how he and C-21 survived their journey beyond the walls of the Dome… Anyway, I ceased reading at that point and turned the files over to the Board. It is not for me to decide what is true or what is punishable.

Fortunately, the launch of the Recruitment strategy is imminent.

Twelfth Report – 2 Days Before Launch

The Engineer has been taken in for Psychological Evaluation by directive of the Board. His demeanour is now placid. He is punctual, focussed; I have not noticed any further aberrations in his behaviour. The Recruitment Pack is on track for delivery. The rocket is nearly complete. A shining metal casing, awaiting the corrected documents, the final touches, before its launch two days from now.

The Engineer himself is like that; there is something peculiar, empty, about him. His expression strikes me; it is as though I recognise it. It is the face the feeling, the swimming-hunger, would wear if it were human. I'm not sure that makes sense. In fact, I am sure I am not being at all rational. Still, I vowed to record everything, and if we are to avoid this sickness spreading, surely we must understand it. It is spreading in me every day, I fear – all the way to my fingertips as I type this, as though I too were a metal casing, echoing, waiting…

Thirteenth Report – 0 Days Before Launch

If I have been successful, these documents are now in your hands – you, foreign ancestor, resident of the mother planet, archaic Employee of Earth. Are you an Employee? Or something else – a citizen, a follower, a comrade – what do you call yourself?

I have smuggled the whole account of my surveillance assignment into the Recruitment Pack, along with this last, likely my very last, report. What is my intention? To atone? No, for while you may from your old-world moralistic perspective think I feel guilty, and perhaps I do, for my part in the Termination of C-21, or the removal of the Engineer's own defiant documents from this very vessel, I do not seek forgiveness. I don't believe in any punishment or reward outside the bounds of OneCorp, and such punishment I will only receive for this very message, this singular transgression – not for following my directives in the observation of the Engineer. No, I seek something far more painful, more impossible, more worthy of the risk. I want to know you. I want to ask you a question.

Oh, backwards Earth colleagues – are you as lonely as we are? Are you aware of your loneliness, the way I never was before these last three weeks? Do you cherish it? Have you found ways to sate your swimming-hunger? Does it ever fade, or wane only to wax again, as between meals? Do your governments, your religions, help? Do your families, your chosen lovers, your greedy possession of each other, of yourselves, of your children? Do your Art-Works? How do you cope, colleagues, what do you hope for? Is it permitted? Is it forced upon you? Are you beholden to the emptiness, as we are to staying full, to erasing the spaces between one another?

What do you do with it – all that space?

Does it hurt?

Is it beautiful?

The Integral – True Literature – Everything Is Blooming

Sofia Samatar

The Integral

Each of us hopes to discover something monumental about the past. The life of an archaeologist is not glamorous; we sift through masses of records, most of them nearly identical, immersing ourselves in a fearsome and idiotic babble. "Taylorism! The One State! Sexual Hygiene!" – you know the sort of thing. Yet our drudgery is justified by hope. Imagine the excitement of discovering, in the monotony of the archives, a sudden, unmistakable flash of life!

The notes I bring you tonight, culled from a badly damaged document found in a charred locker beneath the walls of the Old City, will not, perhaps, strike you as a great discovery. I cannot claim to have unearthed a book with the historical significance of D-503's journal. My artifact contains no information about the Founder; it was compiled long before her time, even before the Two Hundred Years' War. Still, I hope you will find some edification in my notes, which trace the story of a little life – one might even say a failed life, a sick life. As my subject's name is unknown, I refer to him by his nickname: the Englishman.

The story of the Englishman comes to us through a series of fragments. The pages exhibit several different forms of type, and seemed to have been collected from various volumes. Both fire and water have damaged them. They are immensely old, as evidenced by a large number of archaisms ("Bolshevik," "England," "dacha," and so on). They tell of a man in conflict with something stronger than himself, something that perpetually sought to confine him and limit his actions, a threat whose nature is still unclear: was it a geological phenomenon, a political organization, a machine? For the time being, I call it the Integral.

I don't mean to suggest that our Englishman was menaced by *the* Integral – the monstrous spaceship intended to export the doctrine of the One State through the universe. He was one of the Ancients; his era is much older than that of D-503, the builder of the Integral, who came so close to joining the Founder in her escape from the Old City. But the force that stalked the Englishman was something like the Integral: vast, mathematically regular, beyond appeal. It was a leveller and a thing of locks. Again and again he found himself trapped, walled in or out, imprisoned, exiled.

Whatever the nature of this powerful glass monster, it followed him all his life. It was not restricted to any historical period or system of government. Twice the Englishman suffered solitary confinement in the same prison, indeed in the same hallway of that prison, but under two different regimes. "It's amusing, isn't it?" he wrote to a friend – "that I was imprisoned then as a Bolshevik, and now I'm imprisoned by the Bolsheviks."

Why this endless conflict, in every era, with every authority? Why could the Englishman find no system that agreed with him? Perhaps a clue lies in his nickname, for he was not English, but adopted the manners and clothing of England after a brief sojourn in that country. To take on a foreign bearing is to insist, if gently, that one does not belong. One is outside the We. Friends and associates remarked on his tweeds, his "little green English suit," the sight of him chopping wood in freezing weather with a short English pipe in his teeth.

In England he had built icebreakers. He lived in the crack and shatter of great blue-white walls. No doubt you recall this trenchant observation from D-503's journal: "There's no such thing as an icebreaker that could break the most transparent and most durable crystal that is our life."

The Englishman's Integral must have been something like this crystal. And he was the icebreaker, the eternal dissident, the explosive. "Explosions are not very comfortable," he once wrote. "And therefore the exploders, the heretics, are justly exterminated by fire, by axes, by words."

Every day I enter the Old City, that massive ruin, with its mounds of splintered glass, its strange smell of ozone and ashes. I descend underneath, to the catacombs, to search for items worth saving in the layers of detritus, the sediment of history. The Englishman's file called to me when I had deciphered just a few lines. I felt the presence of someone who was not a coldly imitative mirror – someone who did not reflect and reject his world, but absorbed it deeply, becoming one with it, so that it was inside him forever.

Consider his adventure with the bag of explosives. A friend of his left it on the windowsill in the Englishman's room. Shortly afterwards, the Englishman was arrested, beaten, and imprisoned. He knew his room would be searched. He could not stop thinking of the bag of explosives. He managed to throw a note through the bars of his cell, onto the street, asking that someone go to his room and remove the evidence. This was done, but the Englishman did not know it, and for months of solitary confinement he dreamt obsessively of that dangerous bag. There it was, on the windowsill, beside the sugar and the sausage. He had absorbed the image; it became part of him. I imagine it spoke to him of the explosive element in himself that would always betray him to the Integral, and that no one could remove.

True Literature

It was during one of his state punishments that he became a writer. This time it was exile: first in an abandoned dacha, then in the provincial town of Lakhta. "It was a year of extraordinary white nights," he remembered, "a great deal of white, a great deal of black." He had written before, but what he had written, he declared, was not *it*. He found *it* for the first time in the stillness of Lakhta, the green summer silence followed by the white winter silence, the isolation, the eerie nights of muted light, the snow.

What was this *it* the Englishman discovered? The records suggest that *it* was a form of explosive, a hazard the Englishman had been warned against in childhood. After he won a gold medal in school, his teacher told him of another boy who had won such a medal, become a writer, and ended in prison. "My advice to you is: Don't write."

From this I deduce a fundamental opposition between literature and the Integral. But there are many kinds of literature, and only one form is *it*: the type the Englishman describes mysteriously as "alive-alive."

> It is an error to divide people into the living and the dead: there are people who are dead-alive, and people who are alive-alive. The dead-alive also write, walk, speak, act. But they make no mistakes; only machines make no mistakes, and they produce dead things. The alive-alive are constantly in error, in search, in questions, in torment.
> The same is true of what we write: it walks and it talks, but it can be dead-alive or alive-alive.

"Poetry is a state service," wrote D-503; "poetry is purpose." He deplored the poetry of the Ancients, that "brazen nightingale call." The poetry he admired was dead-alive. In the Englishman's file we find a defense of the primeval literature destroyed by the One State. This vindication of a lost music moves me deeply. In the Englishman's words, I catch the flavour of the poetry the Founder might have loved, a literature incinerated by machines, or surviving outside the walls, or revived (as I hope) in our own time. Is it possible that we have coaxed this literature back to life, as we have restored and nurtured our forest home? These walls about us — gnarled and shaggy branches of living trees — suggest that a nightingale poetry might live here, though it would perish in a glass cage. I am no poet, but when I stroll our swinging bridges in the evening after a day toiling under the walls of the Old City, when I hear soft snatches of song from open doorways lit by the furry glow of lamps, I feel that our world is alive-alive. It is the world of the Founder's desire, the one she fought for after her torture in the terrible Bell Jar of the One State. When her friends rescued her from prison, when they dragged her away into hiding, they were already dreaming of this place.

The Englishman dreamt of it too. And perhaps this is the value of my discovery: it offers a glimpse of ourselves before we existed, of our world when it was nothing but a thought. The true writer, the Englishman believed, "works *only* for the distant future, never for the near future, and never for the present." He wrote for what he had never known, what he could only imagine. "A literature that is alive does not live by yesterday's clock, nor by today's, but by tomorrow's." Perhaps this is why he was always embattled, in error, in search, in torment. He didn't belong to his own time. He belongs to ours.

Everything Is Blooming

Yet to claim him as ours – isn't this to cage him, in a sense, to lock him into place, to dampen his explosion? I came here tonight determined to prove the significance of my findings, fearing that these soiled and crumbling pages would leave you cold. But surely pride in the monumental was a feature of the One State. Perhaps the search for greatness is a legacy of the world we have left behind. Friends! I am inspired to propose to you a new archaeology: an archaeology of fragments, of sickness, of the small.

"You, the readers of these records," wrote D-503, "no matter where you are, the sun is still above you. And if you've ever been sick like I am now, then you know what the sun is like." He wrote this during his brief period of inner turmoil, when he knew and loved the Founder, when he came close to following her call. In the end, he betrayed her. But we, who inhabit her living dream – we know what the sun is like! We know the trees like candles, the brilliant light, the mute green fountains of the leaves – all the irrational, chaotic, buzzing world of plants, birds, and animals excluded from the Old City. We are the children of sickness. Shouldn't we value insignificance? Consider the words of the traitor D-503 when he was closest to us: "I am imprudent, I am sick, I have a soul, I am a microbe. But what if blooming is a sickness?"

I became an archaeologist not from ambition but from love. As a child, during the Ritual Readings of D-503's journal, I always listened carefully for the scenes that took place in the Ancient House, the museum so dear to the Founder. She would go there, where no one went, into that dark and fragile structure, the disorder of the immemorial apartments. She touched the colourful bindings of old books, the bust of Pushkin. She dressed herself in a light, antique frock of saffron-yellow silk. Why this performance, this childish play? She was silly and heroic, like the Englishman in his tweeds, with his affected little pipe. This was her favourite place, the Founder told D-503. "This is the most ridiculous of all their apartments."

When she was alive, the Founder was no one — a ludicrous fragment of humanity, trampled, squashed, and thrown away. And the Englishman was the same. He died in exile. In his last letter, he wrote: "The dull light of Paris in February. Some sort of noxious greyness is creeping into the room through the window. If I were a dog — I'd be howling with misery." If he is one of us — if he is, in some way, ours — it is not because he thought as we do but because he was small. He was as trivial as each of us: slight as a seed, a thought, a number. He reminds me that, as the Founder said, the final number does not exist.

I conclude, then, with some stray, embedded fragments from my notes — images more precious to me than any philosophy. These jottings are random, pointless. And perhaps for that very reason, they seem to me to contain what the Englishman called *it*. Reading them, I feel like the Founder in the Ancient House, drinking a poison-green liqueur from a tiny glass. Yes — when I read these words I feel that the Earth itself is drunk, joyful, and floating, and that everything is blooming.

First fragment, like a hole cut in a thick, dark curtain:

An airy, transparent August morning. Distant, limpid peal of the bells from the monastery. He walks past the front garden, carrying his school bag, upright under the gaze of his mother and sisters at the window. He is wearing long trousers for the first time.

Another fragment:

Summer. A smell of medicine. His mother and aunt hastily close the windows and the balcony door. Pressing his nose to the windowpane, he sees a man in a white robe driving a wagon covered with white cloth, under which bodies are writhing. Cholera.

And another:

A crowd. A church, blue smoke, chanting, lights. The cries of a woman in a seizure sound to him like the barking of a dog. He is carried outside. Suddenly he's alone, his parents have vanished. He sits in the sun on a gravestone, crying bitterly.

One more:

A dining room with an oilcloth-covered table. On the table, a dish with something strange, white, and gleaming inside. Miraculously, the white stuff disappears! It's a fleck of the unknown world: his first snow. "And that marvellous snow is with me to this day."

Curtis, Julie A. E. *The Englishman from Lebedian: A Life of Evgeny Zamiatin* (1884 – 1937). Boston: Academic Studies Press, 2013.

Zamyatin, Yevgeny. *A Soviet Heretic: Essays by Yevgeny Zamyatin*. Edited and translated by Mirra Ginsburg. Chicago: University of Chicago Press, 1970.

—. *We*. Translated by Clarence Brown. New York: Penguin, 1993.

ABOUT THE STORIES

Aliya Whiteley
on
'Intrinsic – Extrinsic – Terrific'

I first read *We* a couple of decades ago. I thought about it, I tried to work out what I thought about it, I thought about it, I carried on with the business of being alive, I thought about it, I thought about it, I thought about it. Eventually I decided I'd try reading it again just so I'd stop thinking about it.

That didn't work.

I'm still thinking about *We*. It's one of those books that I wouldn't call a favourite. It's been working away on a deep level for a really long time, coming back to me and returning certain images to my mind, such as a city of apartment buildings constructed of glass, and the one ancient opaque house that contains secrets within. Sometimes I think about the emotions instead: of how it would be to live as a number, and order assignations with other numbers through a ticket system. But mainly I think back over the way it rubs together art, science, achievement, longing, desire, morality, and the continuous need to *improve*. Whatever that means. Am I improving? Are we?

All this makes me uncomfortable. Other dystopias feel more established as perfect, polished systems that end up delivering cruelty by their rigidity. That means rooting for the downfall of the system is the end point to be desired, so there is freedom to begin again. *We* is awkward in the way it depicts oppression, carried out by the very people who suffer under it. It's not a story of defined good and evil as end points, but of why such systems exist, and how they grow, shrink, change.

I knew I wanted to write a story for this anthology that captured the bristling, unsettled feeling the novel had sustained in me for all these years when it comes to the effecting of change. I took the images that had stuck with me, and combined them with the elements that had played through my thoughts often. People are in flux, and so is what they want from the system they live within.

I read *We* yet again recently, and found that some things don't change. I'm still thinking about it.

R.T. Ester
on
'Engine – The Blast – Antiques for Okras'

In Yevgeny Zamyatin's *We*, the spaceship Integral is being built with the intent of spreading the ideology of the United State to societies elsewhere in the cosmos. The Integral exists as an edifice of the United State in both a physical and societal sense. It is being built using the same mathematical principles that inspired the table of hours, which in turn is integral to the functioning of the United State. Wherever the Integral makes landfall, its goal, in a way, is to reshape the society it finds there in its own image.

The titular engine in 'Antiques for Okras' pulls the story into the realm of faster-than-light travel and, in doing this, attempts to make a point about the society we have now and the impossible edifice of capitalism, which in its neoliberal phase, seems intent on accelerating its contradictions. The unnamed narrator, tending to ramble in a manner that mirrors D-503's journal entries, recounts her life in a time when the stars are no longer visible and chickens have begun to lay okras in addition to eggs. Central to both anomalies is an engine built before her time to power a ship that would take its billionaire owner to the stars, but at a cost that ends up reshaping the world it leaves behind both physically and at the societal level.

Any technology will reflect the society that built it, and, to varying degrees, its usage will reshape society in turn. This includes the society that built it and the places that technology and its byproducts are exported to. In Zamyatin's *We*, the Integral is valued for both its function and its symbolism as an integrating force; something that will accelerate the development of societies it comes in contact with until they become hard to distinguish from the society that produced it. From a techno-determinist standpoint, it is similar to the monolith from *2001: A Space Odyssey* in its ability to transform a society by simply coming in contact with it. The determinism of 'Antiques for Okras' is evident in the crises that stem from the engine's construction. We never know whether or not the ship it powered reached its destination, but we see its society-altering effects back home, and in the end, we see a yearning for a new type of engine that will reflect a new and more inclusively utopian society.

Adrian Tchaikovsky
on
'Obstructive Nodes – The Etiquette of Complaint – A Pest Problem'

Zamyatin, like other social dystopian writers, sees the ills in today, and projects them into a future where they are magnified into an almost phantasmagorical excess. The depersonalisation, the lack of privacy, the subjugation of the self. Like other classic stories of a cautionary future or a twisted present, like the work of Kafka and Orwell and Atwood, *We* is a story born of real and immediate anxieties.

This piece, then, is what came to me when combining the evils that Zamyatin wrote about, and anxieties closer to home. The modern world isn't short of things to worry about, and many of the emergent problems we face would have looked depressingly similar to Zamyatin. A world under constant control and regulation by unknowable corporate or governmental powers. The existence of those who actually do the work reduced to mere pieces of a process, unvalued and always on the verge of being replaced by something even more de-personed. Some system or automatic feature that renders us irrelevant and unnecessary. By which time we have already collaborated sufficiently in our own obsolescence that we have no escape or exit.

A society that did not value liberty, privacy or individuality, all in the service of a grander plan that was itself not actually grand, but petty and meaningless, save perhaps to some invisible overclass that might somehow benefit. Zamyatin would, I think, have seen exactly how tissue thin the lies we tell ourselves are.

Anne Charnock
on
'The Earth Heals – Silent Days – Vagaries and Savagery'

I first read Yevgeny Zamyatin's *We* in 2007, and its impact was immediate. At the time, I was polishing the manuscript for my first novel, a corporate dystopia set in Manchester. The main character in my novel, Jayna, works as a brilliant mathematical modeller, being genetically enhanced and augmented with cognitive implants. Disenchanted with her restricted life, she adopts reckless behaviours and encounters new emotions. The working title of the novel was *The Analyst*, but I changed that upon reading *We*.

I noticed the similarity between Zamyatin's main character and Jayna. *We* is the diary of a mathematician, D-503, who discovers love for another human being. Love is an emotion long-forgotten within his world. At the same time, D-503 deplores the "irrational, chaotic world of trees, birds, animals", which exists beyond the glass wall boundary of One State. Looking out one day into this green ocean, D-503 sees a savage, and I was struck by the following sentence:

"But a thought swarmed in me; what if he, this yellow-eyed being – in his ridiculous, dirty bundle of trees, in his uncalculated life – is happier than us?"

I immediately understood that my character Jayna was the polar opposite of Zamyatin's savage living his uncalculated life. So, I changed the title of my manuscript to *A Calculated Life*, and I included the above quote as an epigraph to my novel.

In writing my short story 'The Earth Heals – Silent Days – Vagaries and Savagery' I returned to Zamyatin's concept of a glass wall boundary separating civilisation from the chaotic world of trees, birds and animals. But I decided to flip that world. A devastated, scorched world exists beyond the glass domes in my story while, inside the domes, scientists are preserving the biomes of a temperate climate. And I reference the passage in *We* in "Record Twenty-Seven" in which I-330 climbs a skull-like rock, a gathering point outside the dome, and agitates for revolution to a crowd of naked beings and unifs, saying:

"And you know also that the day has come for us to destroy that Wall and all other walls, so that the green wind may blow over all the earth, from end to end."

George Orwell managed to get hold of a copy of *We*, describing it as "one of the literary curiosities of this book-burning age" in a review for *Tribune* in 1946. He states:

"Aldous Huxley's *Brave New World* must be partly derived from it. Both books deal with the rebellion of the primitive human spirit against a rationalised, mechanised, painless world, and both stories are supposed to take place about six hundred years hence."

Orwell preferred *We* to *Brave New World*. "Huxley's book shows less political awareness." And I am inclined to agree.

Tim Major
on
'Production – Pristine White – Pale Green'

I'm sure I'm not alone in having discovered Yevgeny Zamyatin's *We* only after encountering some of the stories it went on to inspire. For me, Fritz Lang's 1927 German expressionist film *Metropolis* came first, initially as static images in the books about SF I read as a child. Orwell's *1984* was next, then Huxley's *Brave New World*. When I finally came to read *We*, only a handful of years ago, the echoes of these other works were inextricable from Zamyatin's text.

As it represented my first exposure, it seemed natural to draw on Lang's *Metropolis* as part of my response to *We*. When I first become fascinated with those static images of Lang's model city I saw no connotations of dystopia, only a perfect machine. This aspect would later be reinforced by a visit to the Deutsche Kinemathek museum in Berlin, where the meticulous attention afforded to the *Metropolis* city model omits all negative connotations.

It occurs to me that most dystopias are actually utopian for a certain class of people within the story – but you can also step outside of the work to view the *idea* of the dystopian city as a sort of clockwork perfection. Considering the city as a fiction – or as a three-dimensional model – allows consideration of the pleasure of its creator in building it. So, I planned to write about a filmmaker responsible for creating a city like the one in Zamyatin's novel. My filmmaker would invest themselves entirely in the act of creation and would adore what they had made.

I wanted my filmmaker to work independently outside the studio system, which led me back to earlier filmmakers, particularly Alice Guy, who was perhaps the first female filmmaker and one of the first filmmakers to create narrative cinematic tales. Despite her incredible output whilst also acting as head of production for Gaumont between 1896 and 1906, her successful career was interrupted due to her marriage to Herbert Blaché. After emigrating to the USA they founded Solax, the largest pre-Hollywood studio in America; while Guy continued to direct films, Blaché was made its president before their relationship deteriorated. Nowadays Guy is commonly referred to by her married name Guy-Blaché, despite her most important work dating from a time before her marriage, when she was free to work however she wished.

The conditions in which the filmmaker in my story works echo Georges Méliès, the godfather of SF filmmaking. To ensure adequate light levels Méliès built a glass-walled studio on his property in Montreuil, which directly inspired the studio in my story. There are other influences in the story, too, all relating to my childhood love of SF. For example, the detail about pale green appearing whiter than white is inspired by the fact that the original TARDIS console in *Doctor Who* was painted green to appear brighter when the programme was broadcast in monochrome. It's a detail that lodged in my mind when I was a child, and I'm pleased to have found a story home for it.

Anna Orridge
on
'Bittersweet Feast – The Persistence of Swine – To Savour Dawn'

My first encounter with *We* was at university, 23 years ago. As students, we were asked to analyse the text alongside the classic silent era film *Metropolis*, considering their influence on other twentieth century dystopias. What most struck me at the time was its depiction of rationed romance and sex, and the failure of the characters to fully control their yearning for something wilder and deeper in their emotional lives.

When I re-read it in my forties, I found one particular, fairly minor element of the worldbuilding struck me – the depiction of food. It is mentioned, almost off-hand, that sustenance in OneState is all made of petroleum. This seems absurd to a twenty-first century reader, but at the time *We* was written, petroleum products were becoming ever more ubiquitous, their applications seemingly limitless, so it would have been far more plausible.

Since food is central to the identity and vibrancy of so many cultures, it makes sense that a totalitarian regime would seek to suppress it as a form of expression and enjoyment, alongside the arts. As a sustainability professional, I'm painfully aware that many of the fertilisers our increasingly fragile food system is dependent on are synthetic. Zamyatin almost got it right.

My story is set in the world of *We*, exploring in a little more depth at how food could be stripped of its sensory pleasures, and what that might do to those deprived of that vital element of human experience. I hope you enjoy it.

Douglas Thompson
on
'In Praise Of TwoState – Epiphanies –
The Morning After'

I first read Zamyatin's *We* in 2008 in a holiday house on Scotland's West Highland coast near the village of Poolewe. The location is noted for Inverewe Gardens, a real living utopia of a kind, a semi-tropical botanic garden somehow cultivated by a Victorian eccentric on a rocky peninsula as barren as the moon before he got there. It was rather a clapped-out old house, covered in cobwebs. On rainy days I would sit in the house's breezy "conservatory" with a tartan blanket on my lap, until at nightfall when the weather cleared and the roads quietened I would lift my binoculars and spy the mystical red shapes of small groups of deer coming down to drink from the river. *We* captivated me, for its clarity and vitality.

One of my strongest reactions upon finishing the book, apart from exhilaration at having read something so strong and perfect, was anger at George Orwell. It seemed apparent to me that the man had shamelessly ripped the book off while having, I would later discover on the web, the temerity to level criticisms at it in his own review published in *The Tribune* in 1946. I read *1984* at school and had always felt dissatisfied with it. A towering piece of political satire it may be, something that has changed the very language of democratic debate, but it has never actually been in my opinion, a *good novel*. Its understanding of human relationships is too paltry, its empathy with the mundane and emotional: grudging. To me it is a book cold with the political calculation of the very theorists that Orwell seeks to deconstruct.

I re-read *We* last year, the same copy, the same translation. I was surprised that it struck me as almost a different book from how I'd remembered it. Much less serious, more flippant and exuberant, like watching some kind of Flash Gordon movie from the era of silent films. Where *1984* is plodding, stolid and deeply depressing, *We* manages to be full of life and humour. But the target of its satire: Soviet-style command-economies with their eyes set on conquering the moon, are increasingly passing from memory. Therefore I set my own brief thus:

> While other writers shall, I expect, postulate future societies in mind-bending detail, I wish to offer a contrasting flavour: our own contemporary society retold as if it is already a futuristic dystopia. In the hope that such an approach may echo Zamyatin's original intentions of socio-political satire of the regime under which he found himself.

As Ursula Le Guin demonstrates in her essays and novels like *The Dispossessed*: at least in Communist societies people knew they were being oppressed and could think around it in their private thoughts. The worst and subtlest terror of the so called "free world" is that the censorship becomes internalised. We do it to ourselves under the onslaught of social media, which is much more effective for the state and ultimately more endangering to the quality of our intellects.

Nadya Mercik
on
'Buoy – Perfect Citizen – Mother'

We by Evgeny Zamyatin wasn't a compulsory read in my Russian school curriculum. I read *1984* in my twenties, and that's when I fell in love with dystopian fiction. But *We* had always been on my radar. I kept it on my TBR list. Eventually, I brought a copy of the original text with me when I returned to London from my last trip to Russia. And then I finally got down to reading it. I was so stunned by it that I almost straight away re-read it. There was so much in this novel, I didn't want to miss things: the nonsensical-at-first-sight headings, the abundance of metaphors, the narration of a soul desperately struggling to understand the world and himself. Published a century ago, it resonated and felt familiar in the reality it depicted. I guess in some ways it was coming back to the roots; something in between the history lessons and the snippets of my grandparents' and parents' lives. All that packed in a futuristic (for the Soviet time) setting. All so bright and vivid and somehow not outdated.

It wasn't easy to choose one thread of inspiration for my own story. They ranged from singular metaphors – rich in meaning, fruitful for exploration – to bigger themes and world elements. The opaque 'flats' of human heads. Imagination as a disease. The multilegged leviathan. Hour Tables. The impossible last revolution. The lyricism of the three-element chapter headings echoing the poetry of the Russian Silver Age. I was at a loss where to start – the novel spoke to me in volumes, nudging me to see further and go deeper.

In the end, after having the novel percolating in my head for evenings on end, it appeared – almost like that eyelash in the novel. I was drawn to the character of O-90 – a person who seemed to remain in the background, a meek woman of round lines, a symbol of comfort and home cosiness, the last person you would see as a rebel and opposition to the order. And yet when it came to the most important thing to her – love and a child, she found determination and steel in her heart. I wanted to know more of O-90's future. I realised I wanted to explore more of that mother-child bond – what it gives us, how it forms us, how it can, perhaps, be a hindrance. And from there the world of a story was born – the world where these connections were deliberately severed to "improve" humans for the "greater" (read government) good. The world where minds were monitored and influenced. In this world, by some miracle a woman and a girl still had traces of this bond. Not knowing what it is, they were pulled by it. I also had the pleasure of returning to the city of my birth in this story, setting it in a futuristic version of St Petersburg.

I loved every bit of writing 'Buoy – Perfect Citizen – Mother'. And I am sure I will return to *We* more than once.

Liam Hogan
on
'A Peculiar Job – The Wash – Someone Waiting for Me'

I read *We* as a member of the Post-Apocalyptic Book Club (which reads dystopias, as well as apocalypses), circa 2015. I'd already read *1984*, and *Brave New World*, and many others, both in and out of the group, so it was fascinating to see what helped inspire them. I dimly remember the discussion scoring rather higher than the book!

I've often argued that you can tell a utopia from a dystopia from how it treats those who don't fit into the society – and fitting into the society is very much the theme in *We* and others, forcibly fitting, in the scariest of cases. For my story, 'The Wash', I play with that, what happens if people want to fit in, but not all can? If there's a price point, especially for the early adopters? What does getting left behind look like?

Whereas *1984* might be considered mid-stage only the older folk like Winston remember "before", and that proves a dangerous thing to do – and *We* is obviously end stage – it very much feels like there is no before, and possibly no after, it's the early days of societal change in my story, and it hasn't entirely shifted away from what we know and understand, though it's clear that shift is going to be both dramatic and traumatic. *Everything changes*. Here there are echoes of our current hopes and fears for AI! But, just like *We*, and *1984*, stories are not about the society but individuals living within it, so 'The Wash', which contains a fair amount about the mechanics of that shift (it is our narrator's job to help move it along) is ultimately about just two people, bending the rules to carve out a life the best they can.

Fiona Mossman
on
'The Library is Perfect – An Error – Underwater'

I first read *We* when I was studying literature at university. I had taken an extra course on Russian literature, which meant that my encounter with Yevgeny Zamyatin's text included lecture notes on the circumstances of writing and publishing this anti-authoritarian dystopian novel, as well as my usual obsession with the story being told and how it's being told. This was probably helpful for a sheltered wee Scottish girl, but despite the gap to bridge between my experiences and Zamyatin's, D-503's story still spoke to me in a way that was immediate, engaging and thought-provoking.

Returning to the book in order to find inspiration for my story was a welcome return to those days of study and discovery, complete with a mind-map for the themes that I found most compelling: ideas about freedom, crime, perfection, poetics and mathematics, split selves, humans as malfunctioning machines, dreams as pathogens, and throughout it all the desire to complicate and break down the binaries that define and confine us. "Walls are the foundation of anything and everything human" D-503 attempts to argue while despairing about the existence of $\sqrt{-1}$. He's greeted by the laughter of R-13, the poet who knows that building a little wall around infinity will not remove the existence of the tormenting irrational. Infinity is an important concept that comes back near the end of the book when I-330 challenges D-503 to tell her the "final number", demonstrating that just as numbers are infinite, so too are revolutions.

This idea was taken up by another writer who has been a huge influence on me. Ursula Le Guin considered *We* to be "the best single work of science fiction yet written", and her book *The Dispossessed* – one of my favourites – is in no small part inspired by Zamyatin. Here the revolution is ongoing, always under construction, and walls and boundaries move between inner and outer worlds, real and symbolic. Both of these books weave together scientific or mathematical concepts with their philosophical and social implications and their emotional weight for the protagonists in a way that, to me, shows the best of what science fiction can do.

My own dystopia of an endless enclosed library takes inspiration from both of these works as well as Jorge Luis Borges' 'Library of Babel' and Susanna Clarke's *Piranesi*. Control over what stories get told and what knowledge we have access to is one of the ways in which power is exerted. The symbolism of the library (more often seen as utopian, but capable of both) is ready to lend itself to these concerns, where classifications embody worldviews, organisation becomes dogma, and the place of a book on a shelf maps to the place of a person in their social group. Zamyatin finishes *We* with a renewal of the totalising wall, and Le Guin lets Shevek conclude that he will work to "unbuild walls" and let in the draught. Walls, definitions, singular selves and singular shelves might be what we know for now, but knowledge and imagination are both also infinite.

References:

Zamyatin, Yevgeny. *We.* Vintage, 2007, p.37 and p.153
Le Guin, Ursula. 'The Stalin in the Soul', collected in *The Language of the Night: Essays on Fantasy and Science Fiction.* HarperPerennial, revised edition 1993, p.214
Le Guin, Ursula. *The Dispossessed.* Gollancz, 2002, p.274

Ian Whates
on
'Education – The Final Ingredient – The Cost of Living'

I first read *We* in my teens, at a time when I was devouring SF by authors new to me at every turn. I recall being impressed by it as much as enjoying it, and subsequently could appreciate its importance: its influence on dystopian works such as Orwell's *1984* and Huxley's *Brave New World*.

I've wanted to write a story for a while now highlighting the worrying divide that has developed in the UK between 'town' and 'country'. It's by no means universal and such tensions are hardly new, but the divisions seem to have grown starker in this post-pandemic world, with so many urbanites disdainful of the countryside and dismissive of those who live there. That works both ways, of course, with plenty of rural folk happy to dismiss city dwellers with equal prejudice.

The opportunity to write for an anthology celebrating the centenary of Zamyatin's seminal novel offered a framework for this as yet nebulous idea. The story would need to reflect rigid social order, a totalitarian state which relied on control of population and individual. I also wanted the narrative to be sharply focussed, almost claustrophobic in its setting, reflecting the restricted life of the protagonist and contrasting it with the greater freedoms of the visitors (the school children) for whom this is just one of many environments – somewhere they flit into and will soon leave again.

This gave me setting, some ingredients, and the spirit of a story, but not yet the substance of one. Then I saw the actor Timothée Chalamet interviewed on a TV chat show. He was the star of a newly released film *Wonka*, which provides backstory to the classic *Willy Wonka and the Chocolate Factory*. That gave me the ingredient I'd been searching for: a mental switch was flicked, connections were made, and suddenly I knew how to articulate the story.

We may have been published 100 years ago, and the world we know may be very different from the one the book portrays, but science fiction never has been about prediction; its purpose is to hold up a mirror to society and ask the question, "What if…?" In that regard, *We* remains as relevant today as it always has been.

Michael Teasdale
on
'Art-crime – Artifacts – Age of Birds'

I can trace my relationship with Zamyatin and *We* back to the turn of the millennium when I began to make my first tentative steps into online shopping (back in the days when Amazon seemed like a quirky indie project!). At this point I'd been on a run of reading, and in some cases re-reading, the dystopias (both imagined and real) of Huxley, Koestler and Orwell and all sources pointed to Zamyatin's work as being an unexplored foundation on which the latter built the Ministry of Truth.

Back then, I lived in Newcastle-upon-Tyne, a place I was surprised to learn that Zamyatin himself had lived and worked for a spell. There he constructed icebreakers in the Swan Hunter shipyards of Wallsend, just a short distance from the places I would pass, my nose buried in his novel, on my daily commute.

While life has since pulled me all around the world, I have thought about *We* and its haunting imagery many times in the decades that followed. Yet, beyond the Integral, the glass houses and the city of straight lines, it is a particular comment in the book's intended preface that still resonates. Here Zamyatin reveals how "I wrote for those who can not only walk, not only march in time, but fly as well."

These last few years have filled me with dread for the future of art and literature. It is not the rise of AI itself that has been terrifying to watch, but just how badly I feel we have gotten it wrong and just how worryingly we are embracing its dehumanising and dystopic elements over the solutions it should have presented. This technology, which was supposed to liberate us from drudgery and free up time for creativity, now threatens to clip our wings and usurp us in the manner of the novel-writing machines of *1984*.

The story I wrote for this anthology is a reflection of my fears. A place where this timeline could end in a world touched by the mad-logic of the Integral's message. Yet it is also the story of the hope that burns among those of us unwilling to abandon human imagination to the quick and easy convenience of the machine.

I chose the symbol of the bird as the cornerstone of the uprising taking place in my story as a reflection of *We*'s own avian repopulation but also to mirror Zamyatin's message on why we write. As artists and as lovers of the arts, I believe we must not only fly but also bear our talons (or our pencils) against a future that does not have to be as inevitable as we are told.

As Zamyatin said, "There will always be uprisings, revolutions, they are necessary – like storms – so that the sun should become more dazzling."

I'm certain we must prevail, because *art* must prevail.

Ana Sun
on
'Anatomy of Emotion – The Carving of Chance – Seize the Moon'

While our home is not big enough to house all the books we love, over the years we've built up a sizeable anti-library. In fact, I tend to gift away books I'd already read. So I can't recall how long our copy of *We* had sat nestled among our shelves; it had been a leaving gift from a former colleague to my partner, who dutifully read it upon receipt, something I didn't do. The book had moved house with us at least once, migrated along the shelves several times, that when I finally went looking for it, the search took me a good half day.

I suspect I'd put off reading *We* because a part of me feared its legendary influence; I'd known that it inspired books like Aldous Huxley's *Brave New World* and George Orwell's *1984*. As someone who believes that we need more positive narratives to help us come to terms with climate change – and more stories to show us possible, liveable futures – *We* felt very far away from the route I'd taken in my own writing. So, I'd avoided it, put off reading it.

Eventually, it accompanied me to Bristol on a work-related trip. I read it on the train journey, resumed reading the moment my workshop formalities were over, skipped evening social invitations while I devoured it at the hotel bar alongside a glass of wine, inhaled it most of the way through the night – unable to put it down.

If you stripped away the austere, dystopian science-fiction world, *We* seemed to me as essentially a romance – a Romeo-and-Juliet of forbidden love. There are so many avenues one could explore in such a rich world, with its autocratic politics, its rigid rules, its strict social codes – and those who sought to tear it all down.

But very little time had been given to the people beyond the Green Wall that D-503 met in Record 27, that vast outside world which barely scored a few strokes of a paintbrush. So with 'Anatomy of Emotion – The Carving of Chance – Seize the Moon' I wanted to explore how a troubled character might fare in a utopian, future society that lived closer to nature's rhythms centuries after the city fell. It became an opportunity to examine rituals and culture – allowing "old" science and indigenous practices to co-exist side by side with touches of high-tech, where some engineering knowledge had been retained, some deliberately "forgotten".

Later on, I found out that *We* also inspired Ursula K. Le Guin's *The Dispossessed*, a book that's a staple read among Solarpunk communities – and one of my all-time favourites. Utopia and dystopia don't reside on opposite ends of a spectrum; they exist side by side, where one wouldn't have any meaning without the other.

Perhaps I needn't have feared, after all.

Rayn Epremian
on
'Swimming-Hunger – A Rusted Drum – A Ruinous Discovery'

I first learned about *We* during a deep dive into Ursula K. Le Guin's essays and book reviews a couple of years ago. Obviously, I read it immediately. I was amazed by how much the other dystopias I knew well – like *Brave New World*, *Player Piano*, and most of all *1984* – echoed *We*, and yet I'd never heard of it. When I saw this anthology call about a year later, I was eager to try my hand at an homage of my own. One of the things that intrigued me about *We* and its progeny was how the element of sex was used repeatedly, but in different ways and from different perspectives – sometimes a key to freedom, other times a tool of subjugation. For 'Swimming-Hunger' I chose to explore this concept from an asexual perspective. I wanted to interrogate not only how romance might appear to an ace character living in this kind of dystopia, where sex is scheduled but companionship is a myth, but whether the discovery of loneliness could be as potent as the discovery of desire – or in fact be the same thing: the recognition of longing as an awakening of imagination. A revolutionary experience, painful but liberating – and embodied, even in the absence of sexual attraction. I had enormous fun imitating the tone and structure of *We*, following many of the same story beats but from the perspective of the spy. I set my dystopia in a corporate colony on Mars, because the corporate campus, if not corporation-state, is rapidly becoming one of the dystopias of our time – as Octavia Butler warned us thirty years ago. We've learned to measure ourselves by our yield so that we don't have time to yearn. But perhaps there can be power in acknowledging our loneliness, allowing ourselves to imagine the kind of connection we truly crave, and reaching for it, however we can.

Sofia Samatar
on
'The Integral – True Literature – Everything Is Blooming'

I'm not sure when I first came across Zamyatin's *We*. I feel it was always hovering somewhere in my consciousness, often mixed up with another book, such as Orwell's *1984*, Huxley's *Brave New World*, or Ayn Rand's *Anthem*. But *We* is in a class of its own. When I taught it for the first time in a college course on dystopian literature, I was amazed by its quirkiness and freshness. There's a playfulness and wonder to its use of elements that have now become common tropes in science fiction – walled cities, numbers for names, surveillance, and so on. Of course, there's also a strong sense of tragedy and political despair. I became fascinated by the figure of Yevgeny Zamyatin, who created, out of deep frustration and suffering, this story that manages to float beyond its subject matter, buoyed by inventiveness, irony, and charm.

For my story, I imagined that Zamyatin's own papers had been archived in his imaginary city. Perhaps they were lodged in the Ancient House, the museum in *We*, a favourite spot for the rebellious I-330. My story takes place long after the events of Zamyatin's novel; I imagine that I-330 escaped and founded a new society outside the walls. My narrator is an archaeologist who has discovered Zamyatin's papers in the destroyed city and is defending their value to other members of the community. In reality, Zamyatin is the creator of this whole world, but in my story he's a nameless nobody, a minor figure from the distant past.

What's valuable about an ordinary little life? This question, which preoccupies my archaeologist, is in tune with Zamyatin's attention to detail and his defense of the human right to be unproductive, weak, and sick. It was a rich experience to read Zamyatin's essays and autobiographical writings for this story. I came away with a fuller impression of this artist, who was not only an influential science fiction writer but an uncategorizable revolutionary, an incorrigible eccentric, and a clear-sighted poet of small things.

THE AUTHORS

ANNE CHARNOCK's writing career began in journalism and her articles appeared in *New Scientist, The Guardian, International Herald Tribune* and others. She has written four novels: *A Calculated Life, Sleeping Embers of an Ordinary Mind, Dreams Before the Start of Time* and *Bridge 108*. Her debut, *A Calculated Life*, was shortlisted for the Philip K. Dick Award and The Kitschies (2014). *Dreams Before the Start of Time* won the Arthur C. Clarke Award (2018) and was shortlisted for the BSFA Best Novel Award in the same year. Her novella, *The Enclave*, won the BSFA Short Fiction Award (2017). Anne's short stories and non-fiction have been published in anthologies including *2084* (2017), *Best of British Science Fiction 2017* and *2020*, and *Writing the Future* (2023). Anne lives on the Isle of Bute, Scotland.

RAYN EPREMIAN is a writer, poet, and filmmaker who likes mixing sci-fi and fantasy and disrupting other binaries. Rayn has publications in *Liminality* and *Fusion Fragment*, an MSc in Evolution of Language and Cognition, and was a 2022 All3Media New Voices Awards nominee for TV Drama. Rayn currently lives in London and you can follow their work at www.raynepremian.com.

Originally from Nigeria, R.T. ESTER moved to the United States in 1998 and, catching the creative bug early on, studied art with a focus on design. While working full time as a graphic designer, he began to write speculative fiction in his spare time and since then, has had stories published in *Interzone* and *Clarkesworld*. His debut novel, *The Ganymedan*, is due out Fall 2025 from Solaris Books.

LIAM HOGAN is an award-winning short story writer, with stories in *Best of British Science Fiction* and in *Best of British Fantasy* (NewCon Press). He helps host live literary event Liars' League and volunteers at the creative writing charity Ministry of Stories. More details at http://happyendingnotguaranteed.blogspot.co.uk

TIM MAJOR is a writer and freelance editor from York. His books include *Snakeskins* and *Hope Island*, three Sherlock Holmes novels, short story collection *And the House Lights Dim* and a monograph about the 1915 silent crime film, *Les Vampires*. His novel *Jekyll & Hyde: Consulting Detectives* will be published in September 2024. Tim's short fiction has appeared in numerous magazines and anthologies, and has been selected for *Best of British Science Fiction*, *Best of British Fantasy* and *The Best Horror of the Year*. Find out more at www.timjmajor.com

NADYA MERCIK is a writer and literary translator based in London. She is also a member of the British Fantasy Society and an assistant editor of BFS *Horizons* magazine. When not working on stories, she takes long strolls around London, connects to her body on a yoga mat or crochets fluffy things. Her recent passion is taking Japanese Sword lessons.

FIONA MOSSMAN (she/her) is a writer from the Scottish highlands. She is obsessed with short stories, folklore, philosophy and kindness. She has studied literature and book history and works as a librarian in Edinburgh. Her writing can be found in *The Bureau Dispatch, Crow & Cross Keys*, the *Creatives* series from the Scottish Mountaineering Press, the anthology *We Are All Thieves of Somebody's Future* from Air and Nothingness Press, and elsewhere.

ANNA ORRIDGE lives in London and works in the field of education and sustainability. Her short fiction has appeared in *Mslexia*, the *Gothic Nature Journal* and the anthologies *Rock Band* and *Rewired*, published by Ghost Orchid Press. Her essay, 'Bihexuality in The Craft' is published in the Off Limits Press anthology *Divergent Terror*. Her most recent story 'The Moon Doth Shine' won the 2023 XR Solarpunk showcase. Go to @orridge_anna on Twitter or @anna-orridge.bsky.social on Bluesky to discover more about her creative work and activism.

SOFIA SAMATAR is a writer of fiction and nonfiction, including the World Fantasy Award-winning novel *A Stranger in Olondria*. Her works range from the memoir *The White Mosque*, a PEN/Jean Stein Award finalist, to *The Practice, the Horizon, and the Chain*, a science fiction novella about universities, prisons, and breath. Samatar is Roop Distinguished Professor of English at James Madison University, where she teaches African literature, Arabic literature, and speculative fiction.

ANA SUN writes speculative fiction from the edge of an ancient town in the south-east of England. She spent her childhood in Malaysian Borneo and grew up living on islands. One of her earliest Solarpunk stories earned her a Utopia Award nomination. In another life, she might have been a musician, an anthropologist – or a botanist obsessed with edible flowers. Her featured stories can be found at https://singingtotigers.com/.

ADRIAN TCHAIKOVSKY is a British science-fiction and fantasy writer known for a wide-variety of work including the *Children of Time, Final Architecture, Dogs of War, Tyrant Philosophers* and *Shadows of the Apt* series, as well as standalone books such as *Elder Race, Doors of Eden, Spiderlight* and many others. *Children of Time* and its series has won the Arthur C Clarke and BSFA awards, and his other works have won the British Fantasy, British Science Fiction and Sidewise Awards.

MICHAEL TEASDALE is an English author and member of the SFWA. His work can be found in anthologies by Air and Nothingness Press, Tyche Books and World Weaver Press. His stories have also appeared in the pages of *Shoreline of Infinity* and *Wyldblood Magazine* with audio adaptations of his work appearing via Havok Story Podcast and The Other Stories. He lives in Transylvania, Romania with his partner and three cats and can be followed on social media @MTeasdalewriter

DOUGLAS THOMPSON is a former Chair and Director of the Scottish Writers Centre and has published more than 20 short story collections and novels from various publishers in the UK, Europe and the Americas, including *The Brahan Seer* from Acair Books (2014) and most recently *Stray Pilot* from Elsewhen Press (2022). He won the Herald/Grolsch Question Of Style Award in 1989, 2nd prize in the Neil Gunn Writing Competition 2007, and the Faith/Unbelief Poetry Prize in 2016. John Clute's entry for Douglas Thompson in the encyclopaedia of Science Fiction states: "*Thompson is an author of wild imagination who seems able to contain it, and who may write some important fiction as a consequence of that.*" https://douglasthompson.wordpress.com/

IAN WHATES is the author of ten published novels (two co-written), two novellas, and some eighty short stories, which have appeared in a variety of venues including *Nightmare Magazine, Galaxy's Edge, Daily Science Fiction*, the science journal *Nature* and numerous anthologies.

In 2019 he received the Karl Edward Wagner Award from the British Fantasy Society, while his work has been shortlisted for the Philip K. Dick Award and on three occasions for BSFA Awards. He is a director and former chair of the British Science Fiction Association and has been a judge for both the Arthur C. Clarke Award and the World Fantasy Awards. He has edited more than 40 anthologies and is the editor of *ParSec* digital magazine for PS Publishing. In 2006 Ian founded multiple award-winning independent publisher NewCon Press by accident, and continues to be bemused by the fact that the Press has now published more than 200 titles.

ALIYA WHITELEY lives in West Sussex, UK, and has written novels and novellas that have been shortlisted for multiple awards, including a Shirley Jackson award and the Arthur C. Clarke award. Her latest novel, *Three Eight One*, was published by Solaris in January 2024. Her short fiction has appeared in many places. Her new collection, *Drive or be Driven*, was recently published by NewCon Press. She also writes a regular non-fiction column for *Interzone* magazine.

9 781915 556455